RESOLVE
THE CANDIDATE

--- PULLING THREADS ---

Book Thirteen

SHERYLL O'BRIEN

This is a work of fiction. All characters in this book are the product of an overactive imagination. Any businesses, organizations, places, events, and incidents are used fictionally. Any resemblance to a real person, living or dead, is a tremendous coincidence.

WOODWIND PRESS

Printed in United States of America

Mom,

On February 1, 2018, you and I started the Pulling Threads journey. I called on the phone and told you I was writing a story; you expressed your joy and asked to hear a bit. These were the first words of our PT time together:

Kitt Mahoney is doing the two best things in the world—her world anyway.

Since then, I've been doing the two best things in the world—my world anyway. Writing stories and sharing them with my mother.

ACKNOWLEDGMENT

As we begin the final three Pulling Threads stories, I would like to thank my wonderful characters for being fun, daring, bold, humorous, and sexy as hell. You have taken me on great adventures, and have become my dearest friends.

A particular shout out to Fred Serpico, thank you for being the good guy in every story I have ever written, and for letting me plant your ass in front of windows, near and far.

A heartfelt thank you to my team:

Andria Flores ~ Editor extraordinaire.
Nancy Pendleton ~ Goddess of the publishing world.
Jessica Champion ~ Web designer and manager.
25 Hours Consulting

Special thanks to:

Sheila Hannen, my know-it-all neighborhood nurse.
Thank you for checking my medical facts.

Testimonials

"One book will set the hook!" ~ Nancy Pendleton

"This avid reader predicts that Sheryll O'Brien will become your favorite author. She's mine." ~ Ruth S. Bodreau

"The characters draw you in immediately. You will worry, laugh, hope, and love right along with them." ~ Donna Eaton

"There is nothing sweeter than a Sunday morning coffee, a blanket, overcast skies, and a Sheryll O'Brien novel." ~ Andria Flores

"Everything you'd want in a good book. Humor, romance, suspense and great characters! It even takes place by the ocean! Loved it." ~ Helena Green

"I could write a book about the wonderfulness of it all." ~ Faith

"Hunks, humor, and heartache! What more could you ask for?" ~ Marjorie McCarthy

"*Bullet Bungalow* is a page turning family saga and then *Netti Barn* and *Cutters Cove* come along and add a whole lot of trauma to the drama." ~ Jessica O'Brien

"The most promising new author I've encountered in my publishing career!" ~ Jim P. - Woodwind Press

--- Pulling Threads ---

Bullet Bungalow
Netti Barn
Cutters Cove
They Run
They Hide
They Choose

PENOBSCOT BAY
A Rocco Fiancetti Incorporated Investigation

Reasons
Rescues
Resolutions
Torment
Tango
Tests
Resolve

Coming soon…

Revenge
Rebound

~~~ Twisted Threads ~~~

Her Scream

Coming soon…

Stay Safe

Two lovers are gone.

One was shot and left for dead.
One was taken against her will.

Resolve

His final resting place.

Rocco Fiancetti, father of Manuel Xavier, steps from the RFI jet at Ronald Reagan National in Arlington, Virginia. The grief-stricken man is upright—that wasn't the case 48-hours ago. The call he received from Detective Fred Serpico brought him to his knees; the painful news nearly kept him there…

"Rocco. Rocco. I'm sorry. It's Manuel. He's gone."

The detective had much more to say during that call, and he said it, but Rocco registered none of it, at least he hadn't thought so—until he was airborne and headed to the States to retrieve his son's body, that is. He was thousands of feet in the air when snippets of the conversation banged torturously through his head…

"Mike had just left Stacy Remington's townhouse ……. I found Eli Reynolds' name on the military data ……. he was a medic ……. Special Forces

.... Paul Ferraro and Mason Trellis .... Mike went back .... Leavy is gone .... evidence of a struggle .... Manuel was .... Manuel was .... shot .... MedStar Health .... Rocco. Rocco. I'm sorry. It's Manuel. He's gone."

Fred is waiting at the airport with Mike Monopoli and FICA Director John Maxwell for Rocco's arrival. The men have lost a friend and valuable member of their investigative team and each man would be taking some time to sit with their personal pain if they could. They cannot, and the reason is simple. These men are law enforcement professionals, men of action, men of duty. Today, their duty is of the highest form— accompanying a father to his deceased son.

Without word the head of Rocco Fiancetti Incorporated exits his jet and is escorted to a waiting government-issue vehicle by John Maxwell. Anxious energy pushes off the usually stoic John, who barely cloaks his impatience while Mike stores Rocco's gear and gets into the vehicle. The Fed shifts the Escalade into drive before the back door shuts, only to stop it from moving when Rocco touches his arm, "Wait until the RFI jet is airborne. It's delivering The Kid and The Justice to Lewisburg, Pennsylvania." The men sit quietly with their own thoughts watching the jet taxi and takeoff. John gives Rocco whatever time he needs, for whatever the hell he's doing, and when he gets the nod he drives away.

Few words are exchanged on the ride through the historic district of Alexandria known as Old Town, and those that are spoken are in reply to Rocco's questions.

"Where is my son?"

John pauses then pulls a steadying breath. "His body," John pauses again, measures his words, lowers and shakes his head, "Your son has been prepared for flight and is under heavy guard. The FBI has a specially fitted jet for coffin transport which is on loan to RFI for as long as it's needed. Security reasons prohibit me from divulging Manuel's exact location, but he is already on board. After our stop, you three will be brought to him to accompany him home. An FBI team will travel with you. I handled transport arrangements from the departing site and coordinated the arrival times and retrieval requirements with Joy. After the RFI pilot and copilot land at Lewisburg and the current passengers have deplaned, the flight crew will make a return flight to the DC area and assume responsibility of the FBI jet. Once you are onboard, they will fly you to your destination. Joy will ensure that no one is present at the landing site or moving about at The Compound when you arrive. Flight patterns have been shrouded and alternate landing sites have been designated in the event of detection. Rocco, have you made any funeral decisions?"

"Joy and Kitt are handling them. You will all be informed. Until then, there is an RFI team member who needs to be found. I want Hannah Leavy brought home. That is our priority."

John raises his hand to silence discussion. "Men, I caution you about conducting RFI business in this vehicle. There are too many factions at play at this time and I am not able to guarantee secrecy or safety."

The team remains silent until they reach their destination.

FBI Director, Shelby Webber, greets the men at the top of a staircase at her waterfront home. The Meryl Streep lookalike is dressed in a cream cashmere turtleneck, pair of black slacks and black pumps. Though she is head of the most distinguished intelligence and security service in the U.S., the director's current demeanor is soft, approachable, and welcoming, "Mr. Fiancetti, it pains me that we are meeting again under such terrible circumstances."

Rocco nods, "It pains me as well, Director."

Shelby accepts introductions of RFI Detective Fred Serpico and Specialist Mike Monopoli, then leads the men to a farmer's table in the open kitchen area. "Gentlemen, please sit. May I get anyone anything?"

Rocco lifts his hand in silent protest, "My apologies, but could we please handle the discharge paperwork?"

"Of course." Shelby takes three labeled sheets of paper from a nearby counter. "Director Maxwell and I have worked the situation through and have handled all the arrangements for the release of your son. There is a lot for you to read, gentlemen, so take your time."

She hands out the papers. There is not a lot to read. In fact, there are only three words written, "Manuel is alive."

The stunned men are hit with powerful emotion. Shelby walks to Rocco, bends low and whispers, "I'm sorry for the pain recent events has caused you."

Rocco lowers his head, "Director, is there a place where I may have a private moment?"

Shelby leads Rocco to an upstairs study. "Take as much time as you need. I trust all rooms in my home are secure, but I am certain this room is. If you need to make any calls and have any concerns about your phone there are single use burners in the bottom left-hand drawer of that desk." The director turns and leaves the study. The door hasn't yet closed when she hears Rocco address his wife, Joy.

"Mi amore, I have news."

When Director Webber returns downstairs, she finds John and Mike sitting silently at the kitchen table and Fred standing in front of a bank of corner to corner windows overlooking the Potomac. She joins him. "This isn't the time or the place for the discussion you and I need to have, Detective Serpico, but we should discuss The Realm and join forces to bring it to its knees—for good, this time."

Fred nods. "I'll be in touch after Manuel is laid to rest," he continues the ruse with a shake and the lowering of his head.

Nothing is ever final.

Within moments of landing at Fox Hollow Airstrip in Lewisburg, Pennsylvania, Randy Parker, aka Researcher Randy, aka The Kid, aka newest employee of Rocco Fiancetti Incorporated, receives a call from his boss. He whispers to the only other passenger on the RFI jet, "Peyton, it's Naught-Naught-Zero." Randy connects with an uncustomary, "Sir."

"Are you in a secure location?"

"Wheels are down, but we are still on the jet."

"Listen. Do not react."

"Understood."

"Manuel is alive."

The line goes dead.

Lewisburg

Randy and Peyton enter the privacy elevator at the garage-level of 275 Market Street. The vertical ride, as Randy refers to it, will take them to the penthouse apartment of Gretchen Mitchell and Malcolm Price. Randy hasn't told Peyton Wells about his phone call with Rocco. He needs to before they arrive upstairs. He steps near, she steps back. He presses her tight against the wall, leans in and kisses her sweet, bow lips.

"Questionable timing, but that was nice."

He leans in and whispers into her hair, "Manuel is alive."

The ping of the elevator announces their arrival—and also her utter shock.

Mr. and Mrs. Mayor of Lewisburg are sitting down to an early dinner when The Kid and The Justice enter the penthouse. Gretchen squeals with delight then abruptly stops when the look on her friends' faces register. Randy motions for everyone to follow him to the entertainment center.

"What's with all the spy moves?" a very pregnant Gretchen asks, a building concern in her voice.

"I'm freaked out right now and I need to sit in a quiet place. Some things happened, and then they unhappened. There's some not so good news, but there is some good news after the not so good news. Mrs. Mayor you need to stay calm."

"Not likely with all this hoopla."

"Kid, what's happened?"

"The Decadent One, I mean, cyber huntress Hannah Leavy has been kidnapped by The Realm."

Randy stops when Gretchen gasps. He waits for Malcolm to move from his preferred lean against the wall toward his woman. The husband sits next to his wife and wraps his hand around her wrist. He touches her pulse point, feels it pick up speed, "Gretchen, please." He makes tiny swirls on her wrist.

She takes a deep cleansing breath then looks pleadingly to Randy.

He moves to her, sits cross-legged at her feet, "There's more. Manuel was shot during the kidnapping."

Tears fill Gretchen's eyes as she begins shaking her head back and forth. Randy takes hold of one of her hands. "I'm going to tell you some good news, but it is going to sound bad at first, so trust me."

Gretchen locks onto Randy's eyes and nods.

"After Manuel's shooting, we were all told he died. Rocco, Fred, and Mike went to retrieve his body thinking they'd be escorting Manuel home to his final resting place. A few minutes ago, Rocco told me Manuel is alive. He knew I was on my way to break the news to you and I think he wanted me to protect you from unnecessary pain."

"Leavy, is…?" Gretchen halts.

"The team is already working the case."

"How badly hurt is Manuel?" Malcolm asks.

Randy shrugs, "I don't know exactly. Mike Monopoli was the first person on scene and he told Fred that he barely kept Manuel alive before paramedics took over. I'd say Mr. Xavier was bad enough for falsifying forces to be able to fake his death."

"What's the plan?" Malcolm asks.

"Since someone has gone to all this trouble to make it look like Manuel is dead, I think we'll be seeing a breaking news report announcing his death at any time."

My son is alive.

The specially fitted FBI jet has two seats on either side of the flight cabin. In the center expanse there is a for-show-only mahogany casket lashed to an elevated platform. Beyond that is a curtained-off section from behind which a man wearing a white doctor's coat appears.

He approaches Rocco and extends his hand, "Mr. Fiancetti, I am Special Agent, Dr. Gregory Weinstock. I'm in charge of the medical team assigned to this case and have been with Mr. Xavier since shortly after his surgical procedures. I declared him dead as requested by Director Webber. Members of my unit have been the only individuals allowed access to Mr. Xavier since his pronouncement. Until such time as we arrive at your secure location the Federal agents on board this jet will execute the assignment we have been given. There will be no input sought or accepted from you or your associates, Detective Serpico and Specialist Monopoli. Do you understand?"

Rocco nods his agreement.

"If you will follow me, Mr. Fiancetti, I will let you be with your son. Mr. Xavier sustained a gunshot wound to his back, suffered serious internal injuries and major blood loss. He coded upon arrival at MedStar and again in the surgical unit. That event was used as the basis for his death pronouncement. We can go over his medical status in further detail on the flight or at The Compound."

Rocco falters when Dr. Weinstock pulls open the curtain. Manuel is deathly still and hooked up to countless beeping, hissing, and data recording pieces of medical equipment. Rocco takes a minute then addresses the doctor, "May I touch him?"

"His leg would be best. I'll give you a few minutes."

The father places a shaky hand onto his son's thigh. His head bows as low as humanly possible. His thumb begins rubbing back and forth and without realizing Rocco begins counting the slow strokes. He is on fifty-five when Dr. Weinstock steps back around the curtain.

"We have been cleared for takeoff. I need to be with Manuel and you need to take your seat. Once we're airborne you may return."

Fred and Mike are seated on one side of the plane. Rocco nods to the men as he nears them, "My son is alive." He drops onto a seat across the aisle, notices the slight shake of his hands. No words are spoken for many minutes. When Rocco breaks the silence his words are few, but determinative, "Our team will move Heaven and Earth to find Leavy and bring her home. Then we will travel to the corners of Hell to find the people responsible for this act of cowardice. Gentlemen, when we find the guilty parties they will beg to be put down with a bullet to the back."

An ambulance is waiting at the far end of the airport in Halifax. In the dark of night, a member of Weinstock's team gets off the jet, approaches the ambulance with gun drawn and examines the vehicle fully. He then drives it alongside the FBI jet, releases a cargo hatch underneath the plane, lowers a ramp and secures it to the tarmac. Stepping back inside the hull he helps Weinstock roll out Manuel's gurney, as well as the plethora of medical equipment keeping him alive. The agent and the doctor get into the ambulance and leave without comment.

The lone agent left onboard addresses the Fiancetti team, "Follow me." She leads them off the jet and through a gated section of fencing to a waiting van. They get in and within minutes the agent has caught up to the speeding ambulance. "Mr. Fiancetti, anticipated trip time is 90 minutes give or take, is that correct?"

"Si."

"There is a security post in a forested section located off of the main road, is that correct?"

"Si."

The agent places a call to the ambulance, "Agent Hayes reporting in, sir."

"Proceed."

"The transport van is going to pass the ambulance momentarily. We will lead the approach to The Compound. Mr. Fiancetti will need to gain us access. I'll notify you when we are a minute from the turnoff to our destination."

Joy Fiancetti steps from the Computer Center when she receives word that the RFI team is moments out. Joy knows Manuel is alive; she is the only one at The Compound who does. She directs the ambulance to a lower level bay on the backside of the headquarters building and watches as Weinstock's team unloads Manuel's gurney and wheels it toward a suite of rooms. She approaches Maura Putnam, RFI medical director, who is expecting the arrival of a reportedly overcome Rocco. When the real patient is wheeled past, Joy pulls the stunned woman near, "Help keep that man alive."

The physician's assistant packs away her emotions, introduces herself to the visiting medical team and gets to work.

There's something you should know.

Fred and Kitt

Fred Serpico bounds the stairs at the Main Cottage in search of his fiancée, Kitt Mahoney. He finds her in their suite watching over their sixteen-month-old son, Joseph, and swaying Manuel's six-month-old daughter, Charlotte. The Beatles tune, *Oh, Darling* is being sung, a bit off-key, to the sleeping babes.

Fred goes to his woman and places a kiss on her head and one on baby Charlotte's. He takes the sweet girl from Kitt's arms and places her into the crib next to his son then takes Kitt's hand and leads her to their bed. He sits close and wastes no time, "Manuel is alive." Fred pulls his trembling woman into his arms and whispers into her hair, "He is in bad shape, but he is alive, and he is here. John Maxwell jumped into immediate action after the shooting and pulled off one hell of a snow job. He and the Director of the FBI spared no cost and left nothing to chance. They pronounced him dead, locked down his medical care and arranged to get him to The Compound as a corpse. Rocco Fiancetti Incorporated owes John Maxwell a debt of gratitude. His work on this is nothing short of outstanding."

Fred's words unleash a flood of tears from Kitt. He holds her tight and swallows back a few of his own.

Mike and Annie

Mike Monopoli finds his woman, Annie Mahoney-Maxwell, pacing their cottage when he opens the front door. She races to him and throws herself into his embrace. A pixie of a thing, Annie shimmies down and steps onto Mike's feet so she can nestle tight.

"Mike," Annie can't finish her sentence as she is overcome with emotion.

He wraps his arms around her and whispers into her hair, "Manuel is alive."

It takes several seconds for his words to settle and when they do Annie pulls free from his embrace. A huge, cheek-busting smile crosses her face and with a smack to Mike's shoulder she proclaims, "I knew it!"

Mike shakes his head, "Well, you're the only one who did. I thought I lost my best friend and I've been torn to shit over it."

"Are you pissed?" Annie confuses.

"Fuck, yeah. I found Manuel clinging to life with a bullet hole in his back, performed CPR until I nearly passed out, rode with him in the ambulance, and stood in a corner of the

Emergency room praying my ass off when he coded." His voice cracks, "I was told he died in surgery while I was still covered in his blood. So yeah, I'm fucking pissed."

"I'm pretty sure you're missing the bigger picture."

Mike storms back and forth for a few.

On his fourth pass by, Annie grabs hold of his hand. "Michael whatever-your-middle-name-is Monopoli! Get hold of yourself!"

Mike stops dead in his tracks, "What?"

She laughs. "I think you might be in shock—and for the record, that's how I'm going to explain this confusing reaction." She steps into his embrace, "Now, tell me how I can help."

"Just let me hold you, Sweet Annie." They remain in a death embrace for several quiet minutes then head to their bedroom.

Steve and Maura

Steve Phelps is pacing the cottage he shares with Maura Putnam. The RFI detective/sniper is not pacing because his woman was called to assist a supposedly overcome Rocco. Steve is pacing because He. Always. Paces. He halts his movement when he hears Maura open the door.

Before she's fully inside the cottage, he is already asking, "How's Rocco?"

Maura turns a happy face to her man, "He's fine. That was a ruse to get me into medical mode. Wait until you hear the real ruse." As is her way, Maura just blurts it out, "Manuel is alive! He's in very bad shape, but he is currently in the lower level suite surrounded by an FBI medical team that not only saved his life, but has done so by pretending he's dead. I tell you, that John Maxwell went above and beyond on this one."

A stunned Steve plopped onto the couch at Maura's first words and hasn't moved or breathed since. When he snaps to, he goes to his gorgeous redhead, lifts her and spins her around and around and whispers, "Best fucking news ever, Woman."

Maura squeals.

Steve bangs his head back and forth. "Shhhhhhh! If you wake those twins, you own them!"

Rocco and Joy

Mr. and Mrs. Fiancetti lock themselves behind closed doors. He flops onto the bed, she makes her way to a chair across the room drops onto it and loses her composure.

Rocco drags his weary ass from their bed, pulls her from her seat and into his arms. After many minutes he whispers into her hair, "Ah, the emotions have hit. My heart shares your pain over Leavy and relief over Manuel. Mi amore, we will take this night to comfort one another, and then we will fight to bring my son and his love back to us—whole and healthy."

Rocco holds onto his beloved and joins her tearful moment.

Whack-Adoos in the far north.

Gretchen is propped against an explosion of pillows behind her back, and Peyton is sitting cross-legged at the foot of the bed rubbing the pregnant woman's swollen, rag-socked feet. At Malcolm's request the women have turned their focus away from the heartbreak and angst over Manuel and Leavy, and to the shenanigans that took place at The Compound during Randy's and Peyton's recent stay.

"… and Randy calls Rocco and Joy Fiancetti, Mr. and Mrs. Naught-Naught-Zero which they both find quite amusing. Oh, I don't think I told you, but The Kid did his first defensive blocking for Joy when she went places she wasn't supposed to go. The preeminent cyber huntress compared him to a young John Maxwell. She said Randy is highly skilled and aggressive like John was when he first started diving. And Annie Mahoney-Maxwell, the #2 ranked cyber huntress in the world, says Randy has an amazing signature."

"Whatever that means," Gretchen scoffs.

Peyton begins to explain.

Gretchen groans, "Please don't. Instead, tell me what you did while Randy was wowing the RFI team in the Computer Center?"

Peyton gives her shoulder a little shrug, "I was shooting the shit out of things at the firing range and learning hand to hand combat skills at the Athletic Center."

Gretchen throws her head back in laughter, "Yeah, right." She stops laughing when she sees the look on Peyton's face. "For real?"

"For real. In fact, the days at The Compound were the most real days I've ever spent."

Gretchen scooches herself up a bit, leans as far forward as her baby ball allows and studies Peyton's face, "Oh, no. Are you one of them now?"

"Them?" Peyton sheepishly asks.

"The pistol-packing, land-traipsing, covert-living, lie-telling, malefactor-seeking, Whack-Adoos in the far north?"

Peyton shrugs, "Not officially, but Rocco said he wants to talk to me about my future. I helped with a case they are working and he was impressed, I guess. We never got around to having our talk because of Leavy and Manuel."

Gretchen becomes all judge-y, "Yes, well, the events surrounding our dear friends should be reason enough for you to ignore Mr. Fiancetti's call, should it come in."

The Compound

Rocco Fiancetti places a call to Malcolm Price shortly before midnight, "Mr. Mayor, is this call coming too late?"

"Not at all, Rocco. I had hoped you'd call. Gretchen and I are deeply saddened by recent events. May we help in any way?"

"Si. I need the RFI satellite facility at 275 finished yesterday. My team needs to be in America to begin their search for Leavy. I request that you handle the renovations if you are still amenable."

"I spoke with my architect and this is the plan. The living quarters on the seventh floor are all set, so your team can move in at any time. The workspace on the seventh floor will be ready within the month. Until then your team can use my former campaign office on the eighth floor. Manuel and Randy already set it…"

Rocco picks up on Malcolm's fading words. "Si, Malcolm, they already set it as a diving center."

"Yes."

"I accept your offer for the team to work there. Some will be arriving in two days' time. Is that acceptable?"

"Yes."

"Very good, Malcolm. That is all."

Malcolm stops Rocco from disconnecting, "I hope you can tell me the status of Manuel's health."

"My son is under sedation, they say to give his body the time it needs to mend. Several internal organs sustained varying degrees of trauma and have either been repaired or removed. He experienced severe blood loss and passed in the Emergency Room, but was returned to this side of life and kept here by the medical team that is with him as we speak. The cowardly ones shot him in his back. There was concern with paralysis, but it appears Manuel is spared such challenge. That is all I know at this time, Malcolm."

"Rocco, please let Manuel know Gretchen and I are thinking of him and pulling for him."

Rocco chokes his words, "Si. I will touch Manuel's leg for you. Sadly, that is all I can do at this time. My friend, I need to call Muriel Dermot. I do not want one of Manuel's affections to hear the news of his passing as it is thankfully untrue. Mr. Mayor, you should share the truth with your Mama Girl, as she is most fondly of my son's heart."

The truth of that plucks a painful chord. Malcolm Price doesn't bother trying to choke back his tears.

The Realm

The Face

Felicity Ferraro is dragged from a pill-induced sleep by a call from FBI Deputy Director Jack McGovern.

"Did you know about Manuel Xavier?" he barks.

"What about him?"

"He's dead. It's breaking news."

Felicity pushes herself up and turns on the television. Manuel's face fills the screen. She doesn't bother turning up the volume. "Was it us?"

"Don't know. Have you heard from Turner?"

"Let me check for missed calls ……. no, not a thing. How did Xavier die?"

"The talking heads aren't saying which means they don't know. He's been in DC since Stacy Remington's funeral and there was some activity at her townhouse a few days ago, but it's unclear if it had anything to do with Xavier. Sure would be a good time to have Mason Trellis inside the Metropolitan DC police department nosing around, but you got him killed by some Podunk Philly detective."

"I've got another call coming in," Felicity lies as she hangs up on Jack McGovern. She stares blankly at Manuel's face, surrenders easily to memories...

Felicity Ferraro, aka Mrs. Paul Ferraro, aka Irish, was behind closed office doors at the law offices of Preston and Porter. The attorney was not toiling for the firm—she gave up that pretense hours before—she was waiting for a phone call from the head of The Realm. Upon her arrival at the office, she told her paralegal she did not want to be disturbed, so when a knock came on her door she ignored it. When she heard a voice from the other side announce, "Secret Service, ma'am," she stood from her seat.

Presidential candidate Turner Rodgers entered the office and closed the door behind him. "Moments ago, I removed my business from Preston and Porter. I told your senior partners that I can no longer be associated with the wife of Paul Ferraro given he is currently behind bars for his involvement in the Stacy Remington assassination. The senior partners of this firm decided they would rather I stay with the firm. Your employment will be terminated as soon as you and I conclude this meeting."

Anger was quick to find Felicity. The look on Turner Rodgers' face caused her to quickly tamp it down.

"Your unemployment is a fortuitous circumstance for The Realm. I need to scale back my day to day involvement and focus my efforts on getting elected. You will assume the role of conduit. You will deliver directives to the Gang of Eight and report back to me. As of today, you are The Face of The Realm."

The newly promoted associate did not throw a blush, bat an eye, crack a smile, or furrow a brow. Turner Rodgers' words elicited no visible reaction. That's because Felicity Ferraro is a brilliant and ruthless woman who is perfectly capable of being second in line to The Body. Still she opined, "The Gang of Eight will go ballistic."

He nodded. "The Gang will not take kindly to your promotion given they want you gone from the organization. The only reason they haven't made a move against you is because you have the goods on them. I warned them that the 'fixer' always has the goods, always marks a trail, always sets a trap. Individually, you own each of their asses, but make no mistake, Felicity, if they band together, they will break you—then, they will kill you."

Felicity stiffened her back and smiled w.i.d.e. "Please tell the Gang that I am an O'Brennan. If they are unfamiliar with that reference, tell them to research the Irish insurrection known as Easter Rising. Then tell them that they may very well kill me, but they will **never** break me. You might also want to remind them that I have the goods on more than the Gang of Eight," she paused, "and if need be, I will destroy the whole of DC—whether I be dead or alive."

Turner Rodgers took the prick of that slung arrow, "Is that a threat?"

"Of course not."

He began putting her into her place, "Some will question your promotion given your recent fuckups."

She strolled her office, came to a stop at the bank of windows that overlook DC, "Those were Paul's fuckups."

"Not much separation between you two, Felicity. I'd say it's no more than a dick's worth. You need to listen very carefully to the rest of what I have to say." He joined her at the window and blocked her movements. "This is where The Realm currently stands. There is major fallout from the assassination of Stacy Remington. John Maxwell has taken over FICA. His being in the director's seat is worse than when Remington was there. Shit does not get past John Maxwell. He is a problem that needs taking care of at a time when we are down two contract killers. We've got Paul Ferraro sitting his ass in jail, and Mason Trellis with his ass in a morgue. I don't give a fuck about either of them. This is what I give a fuck about: the Dominique and Celia Brettenvue files are not in our possession, and the investigative reporter who's been nosing into my life is not in a fucking grave."

He stepped closer. She stood her ground. He leaned in.

"Your promotion has three immediate consequences. The first is that you are no longer involved in arranging or overseeing contract hits. You are out of the loop. Good news, you won't have to put the hit on Paul when the time comes. Bad news, there may be a day when there are four little Ferraro orphans."

Felicity tried to move past Turner.

"Stay where you are. My eyes and ears inside the walls say your husband is threatening to talk if you don't get your ass to the jail to see him. Paul has become a liability—you know what happens to liabilities. I haven't deemed Paul useless and expendable, yet. It's time for you to get your ass to the jail, find out what Paul plans to do, then do **whatever** you have to do to calm him down. Have I made myself clear?"

She nodded.

The presidential candidate stepped away, "Sit, Felicity, there's business to attend. I called a meeting with the Gang of Eight for tomorrow night. It will be the first meeting that you will conduct. The Gang will want explanations and reassurances. You're only going to get one chance to assuage them and exert power over them, so Don't. Fuck. It. Up."

"I have an organizational question."

"What is it?"

"Now that Tango is behind us, is the main objective of The Realm the same as it's always been? Are we going after Joy Fiancetti, Annie Mahoney-Maxwell, and Hannah Leavy?"

"Yes." Turner walked to the door and stopped. "Convince your husband to shut the fuck up."

Felicity stayed standing until Turner Rodgers left her office. As soon as he was through the door, she dropped her ass back onto her chair.

The Candidate

Turner Rodgers sits on an oiled leather chair in an oak-paneled den at his stately home in Alexandria, Virginia. He is pulling long sips of gin from a way-too-tall glass. It has been days since he's heard from his boss and a slow panic is beginning to churn his booze-filled gut in a very unfriendly way. The wall to wall coverage of Manuel Xavier's death isn't helping his intestinal discomfort or his state of mind. "Remedy, get blind-fucking-drunk." He pulls a long one and as it burns its way down, he gets lost in thought...

He slammed his cell phone onto his desk after the fifth call to Abigail Forrester went straight to voicemail. "Fucking bitch," he growled. He took a quick look over his shoulder at the visiting man. The Senator reigned himself in when The Body spoke.

"Your desperation is showing, Turner. You need to keep your emotions in check, and your dick in your pants." **The man in charge moved from the window, took a seat opposite the senator.** "My plans will not be ruined, Turner. I am in this for the long-haul. You won't be in this much longer if things don't get worked out with Ms. Forrester. The Realm has work to do, and thanks to Dominique Brettenvue, the organization is still operational. We owe her a debt for convincing RFI that the program leaders of our side project, Tango, were the leaders of The Realm. That brilliantly duplicitous move left the Gang of Eight in place and bought us time. I have **no** intention of wasting that time dealing with your fuck ups. Abigail Forrester is a problem. Handle the problem. If you do not, Turner, you will be a problem for me, and we know how I deal with problems."

The Assassin

Layne Osterman is back at Sergeant Noone's place near Blue Marsh Lake an hour or so outside Philly. She's laying low after killing two EMTs who aided Paul Ferraro, aka Boston, aka former Realm assassin on the night he killed former FICA Director Stacy Remington. Ferraro is currently sitting his ass in jail waiting for the next domino to fall—Osterman is waiting to pull the trigger, tipping the next dominos. It's the witching hour and Layne is up examining her sniper rifle. It's part of what the faux Army Ranger does every night—the other part, the best part, is a recitation of the Ranger Creed. Her narration is interrupted by breaking news about Manuel Xavier. She stops what she's doing, sits back, and listens to two loops of the repeat story.

> **Breaking news: Manuel Xavier, former agent with the Federal Investigative Cyber Agency known as FICA is dead. According to sources…**

The contract assassin of The Realm knows deep in her bones that the RFI operative was taken out by someone in her organization. There is no information on how the former FBI agent died, but the seasoned sniper knows it was death by bullet. "When an enemy of The Realm is marked for elimination and suddenly ends up dead, coincidence plays **no role** in the event. Calculation and execution called those shots." She gives a hearty laugh, then sets about staring at Manuel Xavier's face on the television screen, "Sure do wish I'd been called for your mission. You would have been a fun hit," she chuckles.

Dozing off and death threats.

Rocco Fiancetti is locked in thought at a bank of windows overlooking Roseway River. He's been in quiet reflection after spending many minutes at his son's bedside thumb-swirling his affection on the unconscious man's thigh. The father wants to remain inactive at those windows, but the head of RFI pushes himself into action. He storms through the great room, down a flight of stairs, across his land, and into the Computer Center. His team stops working upon his entrance, "Where are we in the hunt for Leavy?" All telltale signs of his Italian accent and kitschy mashups are gone. The former MI6 senior level operative is in full charge. He rolls his sleeves and moves from team member to team member reading this and discussing that. When he is up to speed on the group's efforts he addresses them, "It's time to bring Hannah Leavy home and to end the days of Mathis and Eli Reynolds. Men and women, the clock starts now. Mandatory updates every four hours. Failure is not an option." Rocco holds silent for a few seconds then heads to his computer terminal. He begins his work with a phone call.

Alexandria

FBI Director Shelby Webber and FICA Director John Maxwell are working in the study of her waterfront home when she receives a call from Rocco Fiancetti. John tosses a wave to his boss and leaves the room. On his way downstairs he considers getting a coffee, but decides to stretch out on an Adirondack lounger that's been brought inside for the winter. It's not long before his "take a load off" morphs into a snooze.

"Director Maxwell. Director Maxwell."

He rouses at the touch of her hand to his shoulder.

"I think you might have dozed off, Director."

He immediately stands, "My apologies, ma'am."

"None needed. It's been a very long couple of days. I've worked a plan with Rocco Fiancetti as to which agency will be handling what part of The Realm investigation. I'll go over the agreements with you tomorrow. Right now, I have a few pressing items, so..." She makes a move to usher him out.

He stands his ground.

She halts her progression. "Director Maxwell?"

"Permission to speak freely, ma'am?"

"Granted."

"A revisitation of a former conversation, ma'am."

Her spine stiffens, sure she knows which conversation he's planning to revisit…

"Director Maxwell, are you aware that I removed your predecessor, Stacy Remington, from all cases related to The Realm?"

"Yes, ma'am."

"Stacy continued her work in secrecy."

"Yes, ma'am."

"Director Maxwell. I believe she lost her life because of that work." Shelby stared at John knowing damned well he'd begin connecting the dots.

He got up and moved about—abruptly stopped when he connected the totality of her words. "Ma'am, are you suggesting that Granger Mitchell was not the intended target of the assassin and that Stacy Remington was?"

Webber nodded.

"Director Webber, I want to discuss the bombshell you dropped about Stacy Remington being the intended target during the shooting at the Granger Mitchell estate, and your suggestion that Deputy Director Jack McGovern might have a role in The Realm. That discussion never took place because the shit hit the fan with

Manuel. Pardon my expression, ma'am." He pauses a minute, "Director, may I speak freely?"

"I believe you've established a propensity for that, Maxwell."

"Yes, ma'am. Regarding Jack McGovern, it's safe to say his proximity to Stacy Remington at the Bureau afforded him ample opportunity to surveil her. In our previous conversation you made it a point to say that Stacy was vigilant in keeping ahead of surveillance at her residence."

"She was."

"And that you were quite sure she swept her home several times each day."

"She did."

"You finished that sentence with the word, 'however,' as though there was some area of concern."

"Yes."

John stares her down, waiting for something, perhaps some sort of tell.

"You are wasting your time, Director Maxwell, I do not have a tell. No twitch. No sweat. No eye movement. Nothing. Ask your questions. If I provide you answers they will be truthful answers. Let me put this matter to rest. I pulled Rocco Fiancetti Incorporated off the Forrester and Brettenvue murder investigations and from working The Realm case with FICA because I **had** to pull Stacy off those cases."

Shelby makes her way to the bank of windows and spends a minute taking in the view she loves before continuing. "At the request of Director Remington, I allowed RFI into FBI and FICA investigations. That decision was met with pushback from many inside J. Edgar. When it came time to sideline Stacy from The Realm investigations, the decision sealed the fate of RFI. I couldn't have members of an outside investigative organization report directly to me, nor could I have them report to Jack McGovern since I'd started doubting his allegiances."

John nods. "Understood. You still haven't said what it was that compelled you to pull Stacy Remington from the case."

"I pulled her because of the death threats made against her. Now, if you'll follow me, I'll show you out."

Two empty seats at the table.

After a long day and night of work, and bits of fractured sleep, the team is sharing a breakfast of apple pancake casserole, crispy bacon, sausage patties, and scrambled eggs prepared by Master Chef Annie.

Rocco eyes two empty seats at the table before addressing Fred, "Eat up because you're first up. I looked at your notes and I think there is plenty for you to share. Mike is up after you."

The team drags kitchen chairs into the great room while Fred goes to the Computer Center for a whiteboard and easel. RFI family members take seats in the second-floor loft. Everyone is present except Maura, who is with Manuel.

Fred

The lead detective takes a minute at the window then begins with a Serpico clap of the hands, "We're doing a 20/20 recap. If you could let me run what I have from start to finish before jumping in."

"We know!" is shouted from the group.

He smiles w.i.d.e. at his team, "Good, then there'll be no interruptions." He takes a dry marker and writes three headings and begins.

#1 Stacy and Mathis

"The couple secretly married in 2007. I don't know how long they dated before they married, but I do know their nuptials took place the same year Stacy became assistant director at FICA under Roland Gaffney. This promotion provided Stacy access to the highest level of classified material at the Bureau. Two areas for follow-up: 1) did Stacy become AD of FICA solely because of merit, or did Roland Gaffney want her there so Mathis Reynolds could easily surveil and monitor her; and 2) was Stacy the only person Mathis had or has inside J. Edgar?

#2 Townhouses

"Mathis told Leavy and Manuel that instead of building a panic room in Stacy's townhouse he decided to buy her a panic house next door. That's supposedly why he and Stacy owned side by side units. Real estate records show that he **did not** buy his 'panic townhouse' **after** they married; he bought it in 2005. There are no records indicating Mathis rented out the place after he bought it, so let's assume that being neighbors played a role in their becoming a couple. Now jump to their decision to get married. There would have been talk between the future spouses about selling one or both of their units. Maybe this was when their professions came into stark focus. I'm sure the vocations of these two, being on opposing sides of the law, came up in discussion early on given that Stacy caught the bad guys, and Mathis defended them in court. When they decided to tie the knot, their living together presented certain ethical issues. Maybe one of them suggested they keep their own townhouses, so their work lives could be kept separate. That would have been a solid defense if there was ever a question of impropriety.

"Then maybe the decision was made that their marriage should be kept secret all together. Maybe one of them suggested that since they were keeping separate residences they should build a secret passageway between the two townhouses. Going to and fro between their places could be kept very private and their personal relationship could remain very secret. A bonus for Mathis Reynolds is that the secret passageway could be used by anyone. Unfettered access sure comes in handy if someone wants to plant eyes and ears inside Stacy's office or just hang out there while she's at work.

#3 Eli Reynolds

"He is not a doctor—he is not licensed as a physician in the U.S. or anywhere else. He was an Army medic, a top of the line Army medic, who trained with a ranger unit and was part of countless field missions. That's how he first came to know The Realm's assassins, Paul Ferraro and Mason Trellis. The younger Reynolds brother has sniper training and may be involved with the sniper division of The Realm. I place Eli in the top tier of leadership, but I'm looking at Mathis as being the head of the whole damned nefarious organization. Until proven otherwise, I believe Mathis Reynolds sits at the top of The Realm. He is The Body." Fred makes a trip to the window and talks over his shoulder.

"Let's go back to the shooting at Stacy's townhouse on the day Leavy, Manuel, and I began our work. I was at the window and saw a black Lexus drive by; I told Manuel. Within minutes I saw it drive by a second time; I told Manuel. Leavy entered the room and overheard me mentioning the Lexus. She was walking toward me just as the car stopped. On instinct, I tackled her just as the window busted in. At the time we didn't know the shooter was a trained assassin, so we just thought I was lucky. I wasn't lucky. The shooter didn't want to take me out.

He wanted me, Leavy, and Manuel out of Stacy's office. Whoever arranged the shooting thought that someone would call it in to the Metropolitan police department. If that had happened the cops would have been all over the former FICA Director's house and would have had access to Stacy's office and all of her files.

"Mathis suggested calling the cops, but Manuel and I shot down that idea. This is how I run the circumstances of all this. Stacy has FBI/FICA files in her home office. Mathis Reynolds, aka The Body, wants those files, probably wants her computers, too. But Mathis figured that Shelby Webber knew about those files. After Stacy ended up dead, Mathis couldn't take what he wanted—not without answering a lot of questions to the director of the FBI. Now, if the files just happened to end up in the hands of a high-ranking, gold-badge wearing, assistant chief of Investigative Services for the DC Metropolitan Police Department named, Mason Trellis, who is also a Realm operative, well, that would work."

"Si, it would," Rocco agrees.

Mike and Steve

The reconnaissance/sniper specialist has been seated at Manuel's Steinway piano. He gets off the bench with a touch to one of the keys—it's a not-so-subtle, low note reminder of what is missing and at stake, not that a reminder is needed. "I spent very little time with the Reynolds brothers, but the time I did spend was with Mathis. We basically shot the shit over coffee, and then he got quiet and said something like, 'You were there that night.' I nodded. Unprompted, he said something along the lines of, 'I don't know what happened out there, but you guys are RFI, so I suspect the tactics and planning for that operation were impeccable.' He expressed his notion that anyone who knew how Stacy felt about Granger should have known she would try to protect him, and that the only way Stacy would have lived through that night is if she weren't in that room with Granger."

Mike is interrupted by a groan from Steve. He moves toward his friend and addresses him squarely, "I don't think you'll be groaning in a minute, Steve. I. Want. You. To. Listen."

Steve nods.

"During my original deconstruction after the assassination of Stacy, I detailed the following: 1) I was watching inside the kitchen, and you were watching the shooter. 2) Stacy could hear everything you were saying. 3) My best guess was that after she heard you say the shooter was ready for the shot, she overplayed the moment, or had second thoughts about Granger being there. 4) She made her move to protect him and stepped toward Granger just as the shot was made. That was how I ran it at the time."

Steve nods.

Mike continues, "I've replayed that scene a hundred times. My initial assessment was wrong. I think. I'm 99% sure, give or take 1%, that my initial assessment was wrong."

The room laughs when Mike quotes Manuel, silences when his words register.

Mike smiles wide.

Fred pushes in, "Run the scene, Mike."

"Stacy was to Granger's right, sort of facing him. I thought Stacy stepped toward Granger, but he was the one who moved—away from Stacy. I'm almost positive that Stacy remained fixed and that Granger was the one in action."

Mike is interrupted by a groan. All eyes turn to Steve who has been quietly listening. He begins to shake. He gets up and starts pacing the length of the great room.

Rocco raises his hand, demanding silence from the team.

Steve's pacing turns frantic and he begins clenching and unclenching his hands. "Fuck, fuck, fuck." Steve groans. Steve paces. "Fuck, fuck, fuck." Steve grunts. Steve paces. He walks to Fred, "Stand up you son of a bitch."

The entire room is deathly still. No one is speaking. No one is breathing.

"When you came to Minty's Shack after the shooting and told me it wasn't my fault, and I said it was, and you said even if I made a noise, or fucked up some other way, you said it wasn't my fault because shit happens."

Fred nods once.

"Fred, it **wasn't** my fault. Boston wasn't there to kill Granger. He was there to kill Stacy. I've been replaying that fraction of a second through my head for weeks. That fucker-nightmare holds me hostage. I've gone over it and over it and it never makes sense. It doesn't make sense because I've been running the shit show through the filter of a hit on Granger. Everyone is right—Stacy would have protected Granger no matter what—**and** Granger would have protected Stacy no matter what. He's the one who moved **away** from the woman he considered to be his daughter. Mike, run this with me. Tell me what you were seeing in your scope, and I'll tell you what I was seeing."

The great room goes deathly quiet.

Mike: "As soon as I heard Stacy arrive, I took my sight off of the assassin and turned it to the kitchen. Stacy and Granger walked about half-way into the room then stopped. The abrupt halt positioned them in front of the wall of windows. A second or two passed, Steve whispered that Ferraro was ready for the shot."

Steve: "Stop there. The assassin had a visual into the kitchen. He got shot-ready, sighted, moved his finger to the trigger, lifted his head a fraction, turned his face toward the left and pulled the trigger, without sighting again." Steve begins pacing. "Mike check me on events before the shooting—only stop me if I go afoul. You and I were set in our fire sights. You whispered that the assassin was 200 yards from his lair. When he was set, I whispered that he was mounted. The assassin took his binoculars and scanned all floors of the Cottage, lowered his binoculars and turned his head to the left toward me. Then he raised his viewers again, scanned the woods in your direction, then toward the Carriage House, then back to the Cottage. He put the binoculars aside, checked the time on his watch, went flat on his stomach, inched into place, sighted through his scope, and waited for visuals on his victim."

Mike's been nodding through all of Steve's recounting. When Steve is finished Mike pushes in, "When Paul Ferraro looked in your direction and then in my direction, he was letting us know he'd made us."

Steve nods, "He knew we were there. He **definitely** knew I was there and in the tree. He made me as his opponent. When he sighted his target in the kitchen then lifted his head and turned it my way, he knew I'd read that as a pause in action. That I wouldn't take him out until he resighted. He didn't need to resight because he already had Stacy in his crosshairs, so he pulled the trigger. Stacy Remington is dead because she was the intended victim."

Fred catches his friend who is overcome with emotion and exhaustion.

Breaches, business cards, and babies.

Shelby Webber arrives downstairs to find John Maxwell pacing along the shoreline of the Potomac River. She looks for a boat, "Nope, he didn't use the 400 mile long waterway, and it's unlikely he scaled 30 foot high stone walls with wrought iron fencing. And yet he's on my property." She makes her way to the security cameras, "Still engaged." She checks the outdoor thermometer, "Twelve effing degrees. Shit. I should just leave him out there, but I'd be hard pressed to explain a dead director on my grounds. Still." She goes downstairs, grabs her down coat, throws on her boots, a hat, a pair of thermal mittens, and storms to her intruder.

John feels her approach, "I couldn't sleep. I hope I didn't disturb you."

"You didn't. How did you get past the gate, John?"

"I'd rather not say. If I do, I won't be able to do it again. Besides, it will be good for you to have to figure it out," he smirks as he heads past her to the house.

"I'll just change the access codes and beef it up around here," she calls after him.

"You won't, and it wouldn't help, anyway."

"I'll post agents."

"Still won't help."

John leaves a wondering Shelby at the shoreline.

By the time the director gets upstairs John is rummaging through her kitchen cabinets, "Where's the coffee?"

"In the coffee percolator, just plug it in. Director Maxwell, how did you get onto my property?"

"Director Maxwell isn't going to tell you either. You have a security breach. I found it. You're my boss, you should be able to find it. Do you want cream and sugar?"

"You are overstepping here, Director Maxwell."

"By asking how you take your coffee, Director Webber?"

"Splash of cream, pinch of sugar."

John looks over his shoulder, "Huh, didn't think of you as the fussy type."

"I'm not any type and you are perilously close to insubordination."

John hands his boss her coffee, "Ma'am, I passed insubordination a long time ago."

Shelby nods, "We need to get back on track with the power dynamics here, FICA Director Maxwell. After today, there will be no meetings at my home, so there will be no cause for you to breach my security. Is that clear?"

"Yes, ma'am." John hops onto the counter and sips his coffee.

Shelby rolls her eyes, "Rather juvenile. Perhaps that's why you take up with younger women."

John smirks, "I assume you are referring to Hannah Leavy because she is the only younger woman I have ever taken up with. And should we be talking about this given Leavy's current predicament, Director Webber?"

"We shouldn't be talking about this at all," Shelby says before taking a seat at the farmer's table.

A few quiet moments go by before John hops from the counter and pours himself another cup. He leaves the kitchen and plants himself in front of the windows. He gets pulled by the views of the Potomac and gets lost in thought about Leavy.

Shelby gets lost in thought about the man filling every inch of her headspace...

"Come on in. Have you had dinner Director Maxwell?"

"No, ma'am."

"Good, I'm serving lasagna. I worked from home today and whenever I work from home, I cook.

You're in for a treat—my lasagna is the best, or so I've been told. My sister says that people who find me objectionable invite me to their dinner parties if I'll agree to bring my lasagna. I choose to take that as a compliment. Have a look around the views are wonderful, even in late November."

Her thoughts about John Maxwell back then are the same now, *He is an exceedingly good looking man, especially with a morning scruff that barely covers his strong dimpled chin.* She shivers as she considers his long, lean, muscular body. "And from the cling of his sweater there's a great set of abs. John Maxwell is a gorgeous, athletic man, who most women find irresistible."

Shelby Webber has never joined the ranks of most women. Still.

"Director. Director Webber. Did you say something?"

Shelby's been caught daydreaming, "I'm sorry, did you say something, Director Maxwell?"

"I asked what is taking up your headspace?"

"I was thinking of Stacy."

John smirks, "Well, then, I believe you were going to tell me about the death threats made against Director Remington, the ones that resulted in her being removed from The Realm case."

Shelby sips the last of her coffee and heads for more. "Three envelopes were delivered to my personal post office box. They were numbered, so I opened them in sequence. Envelope #1: A piece of print quality paper with the words The Realm typed in Calibri (Body) 14 font. Dismissing coincidence, I linked the (Body) font to The Body, aka the leader of The Realm. Envelope #2: A piece of print quality paper with a picture of a black outlined octopus. The picture was lifted from the free image catalogue on the web. Envelope #3: Two business cards, one was in shreds, one was in pristine condition. Both of them were Stacy's. The shredded one had been shot, leaving only fragments, still, I knew it was one of Stacy's—I'll explain how in a minute. In combination, I interpreted the envelope messages to mean that The Realm knew Stacy was looking at the organizational structure as an octopus and that she would die by a bullet if she continued."

John thinks a minute, "Something's missing. Stacy is an FBI agent. By virtue of her job she was under threat all the time, so that doesn't account for your removing her. Further, Stacy Remington was the most formidable woman I've ever met. She wouldn't step down from any threat, and she'd be pissed if she were forced to. And **you** wouldn't risk an investigation by taking her off it because of a simple threat."

"It wasn't a simple threat, Director Maxwell."

"Explain."

"The business card put me on alert because the threat was made by someone close to Stacy. This is where the business card comes into play. When she was promoted to FICA Director, there was a printing error on her business cards. They came in on pink stock. Stacy got the biggest kick out of that. She came into my office and said, 'Stacy Remington **does not** do pink anything.'"

John smirks.

Shelby laughs. "You never saw that side of Stacy, did you John?"

"No, but I've been hearing things from RFI team members about the two sides of Stacy Remington. I wish I'd seen that one."

Shelby nods and smiles. "Stacy respected you John. She took your leaving the Bureau very badly." Shelby abruptly changes course when she sees regret cross John's face. "I digress. We were talking about the business cards. Obviously, I had the incorrect cards replaced. Stacy asked if she could keep the pink set. Every year she tucked one into my Christmas card. I'm sure that tickled her…"

"…pink," John finishes the pun.

Shelby smiles wide, "Yes." Her eyes sparkle with unshed tears for her friend. She pushes through, "When I got the envelope containing the business cards, I remembered Stacy kept them in her desk drawer at her home office, so that she'd never give one out at work by mistake."

John is nodding. "So, unless someone got access to those pink cards at the time of their printing, it's a very good probability that whoever got those cards had access to her home office."

"Yes."

"When you took Stacy off the case, wait a second, when did you take Stacy off of The Realm investigation?"

"Informally, when I removed RFI from the Forrester and Brettenvue cases. Formally, the afternoon she was killed."

"Why? Did something happen? Did you identify a suspect?"

"No, but I had a nudge that it was Mathis Reynolds."

"Did you know Stacy and Mathis were married?"

She shakes her head. "Not until the afternoon of her death. For some reason, Stacy chose that day to tell me about her personal life. She said she and Mathis dated for years, secretly married, and they had some sort of secret passageway between their townhouses. I knew, in my gut, that **he** sent the enveloped threats. I should have told her. I would have told her, but she said she was going to visit Granger Mitchell for the night. I thought I'd have time to put some wheels in motion regarding Mathis. I was wrong. Dead wrong."

She never told me about the plan.

Fred has been ignoring the vibrating phone in his pocket for the past twenty minutes. He is desperate to answer it, but he just got his chance to be with Manuel and he refuses to be interrupted. After his half-hour allotted visitation, he heads out and checks his phone, "Six missed calls from John Maxwell. Shit." He presses return call, "John, I was with...never mind. What's so urgent?"

"Director Webber pulled RFI off the case because she **had** to pull Stacy off the case. Webber received a death threat against Stacy shortly before she curtailed her participation in the Forrester, Brettenvue, and Realm cases. The day of Stacy's shooting, she confided that she was married to Mathis Reynolds. That's when Director Webber suspected the threat against Stacy might have come from inside the marital house."

"Shit. We just started circling that drain, John. Is Director Webber with you?"

"Yes."

"Put me on speaker."

"We're on, Fred. Go ahead."

"This is gonna take a few. We were doing a 20/20 session on Mathis and Eli. This is some stuff that came to light. 1. Stacy got promoted to AD at FICA in 2007—the same year she married Mathis. 2. They kept their marriage secret for a dozen years. 3. He said he bought the townhouse next to Stacy's and built a secret passageway so she could escape to his house if needed. There's a discrepancy about when he said he bought it and when he actually bought it. 4. The secret passageway between townhouses was a gateway of opportunity for someone to plant eyes and ears and to rummage through Stacy's office whenever she wasn't home. 5. Eli isn't a doctor, he's an Army medic who served with Paul Ferraro and Mason Trellis. There's more, but this is where things get interesting.

"Mathis told Manuel and Mike that anyone who knew the way Stacy felt about Granger would have known she would try to protect him. And the only way Stacy would have lived through that night is if she weren't in that room with Granger. When Steve heard those words, he had a physical reaction. He got agitated, began pacing and clenching his fists. Then he pulled up short and said that Boston wasn't there to kill Granger. He was there to kill Stacy."

"Yeup, that's what we're thinking."

Fred pulls a breath then continues, "I've got some questions on all of that, but they aren't as important as this question. Director Webber, if you thought Stacy Remington's life was at risk, why did you let her participate in a 'lure and capture' plan for a known assassin?"

"I didn't let her do anything, Detective Serpico. Stacy never told me about the plan. I thought she was going to Granger Mitchell's house to discuss a personal matter with him."

There is dead silence. Fred breaks the silence, "I'm done, John. You can speak now."

"What the hell is there to say, Fred?"

Mathematical improbabilities.

While Felicity waits for her husband to be brought to her, she sits with their last conversation misfiring in her head…

"Shut the fuck up ……. you **think** you are calling the shots ……. you **think** you are The Face of an international crime organization ……. you **think** you were hand-selected by The Body. You don't even know who The Body is."

She still doesn't know the answer to that question. She can tell from the look on Paul's face when he shuffles in that he won't be telling her, so she leads with an equally pressing question. "Who else knows the identity of The Body?"

He laughs.

"Who else knows Turner Rodgers is not The Body?"

He laughs.

"Paul, I'm flying blind out here. The Realm killed Manuel Xavier. I'm supposedly second in command, The Face, the conduit between The Body and the Gang of Eight, and yet I had no idea about Xavier until Jack McGovern told me. What the bloody hell, Paul?"

"You should have bloody suspected a move on RFI, Felicity. I **told** you everyone at Granger Mitchell's estate that night is going to be eliminated. No witnesses. No trial. No conviction. No problems."

"Fair enough, but for appearances sake, I shouldn't be learning about a fucking hit on an RFI detective from Jack McGovern. Turner Rodgers should have told me even if he's stepping back to handle his presidential campaign. He must know these things. Right? He must be in touch with The Body. Right?"

Paul's face tightens. "Be the fuck quiet, Felicity. Turner's boss, our boss, is probably underground. The hit against RFI was huge—if you were meant to know about it, you'd know about it. RFI is going to be on the warpath looking for answers and retribution. The best way to avoid being caught is to go low, so The Body went low. That put the rest of us into the long game, so calm down, keep your nose down, and do as you are told."

"Told by who? Jack McGovern? Does he know that Turner isn't The Body?"

"No. There are four people who know who The Body is. One person is in the Gang of Eight. Two people are sitting their asses in prison waiting for a presidential pardon, Roland Gaffney and Yours Truly. The other person is the one who will be doling out those pardons, Turner Rodgers."

Felicity scoffs, "If he's still alive."

"He's alive. He's probably soothing his nerves with a bottle of gin. If he hasn't heard from The Body either, then he's freaking out, probably even worse than you. Once Turner dries out he'll be in touch. Tell him what I told you: to calm down, keep his nose down, and wait it out." Paul scoffs, then adds, "If there's anyone who should be freaking out right now, it's me. I need Turner Rodgers sitting in the Oval Office so I can get a pardon, or I need every fucking witness who was at Stacy's shooting eliminated. The contract hits might take longer to arrange now that Fiancetti has been poked, but The Body will come through. Now get over here Felicity and help me with my dick."

Drexel Hill
Philadelphia Detective, Ted Brothers, is sitting in a 'freeze your balls off' root cellar in his modified log cabin home reviewing stolen financials on the presumptive 2020 GOP presidential candidate. Detective Brothers did not steal the records, but he is in possession of them, a Federal offense that could send him to Leavenworth.

Penny Meehan, the sole survivor of Paul Ferraro's string of assassinations is also in that 'freeze your tits off' root cellar. She is involved in her own research project, a review of military records compiled by cyber huntress, Hannah Leavy, the newest kidnap victim of The Realm. "Ted, I'm wondering about a mathematical probability."

The man who holds a PhD in Applied Mathematics and Computational Science growls low and long, "Then I'm your man."

Penny laughs, "Yes, but not because you can add and subtract."

"Jesus, Penny, I can do more than add and subtract. I'm a mathematical genius, like a damned walking calculator, like a—"

"Nerd," she nudges.

He laughs big, "Exactly like that. So, what's your question?"

"What are the chances that The Realm contract killer who ambushed two EMTs **didn't** know Paul Ferraro, Mason Trellis, and Eli Reynolds prior to becoming part of The Realm? We established the first three knew each other through their Army Ranger days, so I'm thinking it's more than likely the killer of the EMTs also came up through the military. Statistical thoughts, Detective?"

"Probability that they didn't know one another is unlikely."

Penny laughs big, "That's it? That's your statistical analysis?"

Ted inches closer to his woman, removes his puffy winter coat, lays it behind her, places his hand under her recently unbandaged, unslung, shoulder and leans her back. He is on her, kissing her, and craving the hell out of her in a nanosecond. Until she pulls her lips away.

"Ted. It's obvious The Realm is eliminating whoever was at the Granger Mitchell estate that night, so that means I'm not the only one in this house who has a contract on their head."

Ted pushes up, "Moment gone."

She laughs and offers her hand to him.

He helps her up and dons his jacket.

Penny gets a jump on the conversation. "So, let's recap who The Realm is after. There's me because I snooped on Turner Rodgers and may have come up with something I shouldn't have. She bangs a memory…"

"I headed to the Library of Congress where I hit paydirt. I found the roster for the Class of 1999 interns and plenty of pictures of young ladies and young men rubbing elbows with the Congressional leaders of our great republic. As it turned out, there were two interns in Congressman Rodgers' office in 1999. Abigail

Forrester from Scranton, and Kathleen 'Katie' O'Brien from Jessup."

Penny handed one of the folders on her lap to Captain Johnson, "Those are copies of receipts from my trip to DC: gas station, hotel room, food receipts, and a handwritten record of what I did, where I went, and for the most part with whom I spoke. You can cross check the dates and times that I toured the Capitol—they keep a log of visitors. I only have copies because I attached the originals to my *Kiss and Tell* expense report."

Ted touches Penny, pulling her from her memories, "Where'd you go?"

"I was remembering a conversation I had with Fred and Captain Damian Johnson about my trip to DC, when I was trying to find a connection between Abigail and Turner Rodgers."

"And?"

"I think The Realm keeps trying to kill me because I found out something. I can't remember what it is, but I saw something, or read something, or heard something."

"Do you have notes or records?"

"I did. At the condo. But I haven't been back there since Boston shot me."

"Let's put this aside, get you back on track on what you were saying before. Who else is on the elimination list?"

"There's you, Fred, Mike, Steve, and Granger because you were with Stacy the night of the shooting. Is there anyone else?"

"Not that I know of, so I guess that's the killer's elimination list. Of course, there's the other list—The Realm's original list."

"Original list?"

"The Realm kidnapped Hannah Leavy twice. First time was from an off-site FICA facility called Netti Barn. The abductors took her and tried to ship her off to Peru, but she was rescued by Manuel. And now, The Realm kidnapped her from Stacy Remington's townhouse. Leavy is one of the top three cyber huntresses in the world. The other two are Joy Fiancetti and Annie Mahoney-Maxwell, who are both with RFI. The Realm has wanted all three of them for years. I see no reason why that isn't still the case. I'd bet my cabin that Joy and Annie are on a kidnap list." Ted is interrupted by the buzz of his cell, he reads caller ID, "I was just about to call you, Detective Serpico."

"What about?"

"An elimination list The Realm is working through. Lucky just did a recap of who has already been—"

"Ted, I need to interrupt you. It's important. If you're on a secure line put me on speaker."

"You're on speaker, Fred."

"Hi, Penny. How's your recovery going?"

"I'm working through it. I got rid of the binding and slinging, and I've got a physical therapist coming in three times a week. I'm seeing some progress. Thanks for asking. How are you all doing?"

"That's why I'm calling. Listen up and don't interrupt. Immediately after Manuel's shooting, FICA Director, John Maxwell, locked down his medical care and pulled off a snow job that rivals any I've ever heard of. He assigned an FBI medical team to Manuel who pronounced him dead then worked their asses off to make sure he didn't end up that way. When he was able to be moved, they loaded him and every piece of medical equipment known to man onto a specially fitted FBI jet normally used for coffin transport. He's at The Compound working through a tough battle, but he is not dead. We want the world to think he is, but you guys are part of the RFI team, so you are in on the secret."

"Holy shit," Ted and Penny whisper in unison.

Silence hangs.

Fred breaks the silence, "Did I lose you two?"

"We're here. Words fail," Penny says.

"They never fail me, Penny. I've got something else and I'm sure this one will leave

Ted speechless. Very long story short, Ted, the reason Stacy Remington was killed at Granger Mitchell's place is because she was the intended target."

"Holy shit," the twosome whisper in unison.

Fred laughs, "You two sound like an old married couple. Damn good to hear something nice is happening in this fucked up world. I'm heading back to the States and will be working out of 275. RFI is setting a permanent satellite office there, so I'll be swinging by to see you two really soon and—"

Ted takes his life into his own hands by interrupting Fred Serpico, "Sorry for the interruption, but I've got something in my craw. It's obvious that anyone at Granger's that night is on an elimination list."

Fred acknowledges the point with a simple, "Yeah."

Ted moves on, "I'm sure you've considered my next point, Fred, but what with all the emotional shit going on up there, I think this deserves some discussion."

"Shoot."

"I think there's another list. The Realm has the #3 ranked cyber huntress in their possession. There are two other huntresses. The Realm wanted all three of them the first go around, so I see no reason why they wouldn't want all of them now. Like I told, Lucky, I'd bet my cabin that Joy and Annie are on a kidnap list."

"Penny, kiss your man for me. Gotta go."

Penny goes in for that kiss and is met with the raise of Ted's hand.

"What's up, Ted?"

He paces a bit then stands near the space heater, "Something. Something from that night. It's nagging—it's been nagging, and I just can't grab hold of the thread. It's something about Stacy." He goes back to Penny and takes her hand, "Come on, I need a break."

Are we clear?

     Shelby and John silently work through the ramifications that Stacy Remington was the intended target of the assassin known as Boston. There is quite a bit of pacing across the great room by each of them and some alone time at the bank of windows overlooking the Potomac River. There is no shared assessing of information, no verbal outrage or shock about the husband of a trained agent duping her through marriage and discarding her through assassination. The only thing that settles deep in the two trained agents is a pitiful resignation that Stacy Remington's life ended because she no longer held purpose for the man she thought loved her. Within the silent minutes of personal and professional reflection; tension, frustration, and anger take hold and darken the space between them.

     Director Webber walks to the stairway that leads outside, "It's time for you to leave."

     John remains at the windows with arms crossed. He speaks over his shoulder, "You tried to put distance between Stacy and The Realm investigation. When that didn't work, you took Stacy off the case. You couldn't have done anything more than what you did. Maybe if you'd had more time, maybe if we'd all had more time, Shelby, we—"

"Director. It's Director Webber. And you need to go, Director Maxwell."

John turns toward the woman who's fighting to retain control, "Very well, ma'am." He pauses when he reaches her, then moves down the stairs. When he gets to the door, Shelby calls after him, "Do not breach my security again. Are we clear Director Maxwell?"

"Very clear, ma'am."

The Compound

Rocco Fiancetti asks Fred Serpico to join him in his office, "Shut the door and take a seat."

Fred sits for several minutes, several uncomfortable minutes. He breaks the silence, "Say it, Rocco. We both know what's on your mind."

"I have never crossed the line, in my professional life," Rocco tags a note onto the word and holds Fred's eye a fraction of time before continuing. "If there was an opportunity to bring in a suspect, no matter how reprehensible the malefactor, I brought him or her in. I have no intention of honoring the line this time. When you locate Eli and Mathis Reynolds, find out which of them put a bullet into the back of my son. I will return the favor. Are we clear?"

"Very clear, sir."

Fred calls a meeting in the great room for the RFI team and their families. This time he requests that Dr. Gregory Weinstock be present. After formal introductions of Manuel's physician, Fred begins, "Some of us are hitting the road today. We have a missing family member and we are going to find her and bring her home. Over the next many days, weeks, or months, RFI team members will be rotating in and out of The Compound as we see fit. The traveling team will not be the only team working this case. It's all-hands-on-deck.

"Hannah Leavy has been taken by The Realm. They tried to take her once before, but Manuel Xavier stopped them. Sadly, this time they managed to complete their mission. Men and women, Leavy is only part of their mission. The Realm wants all three cyber huntresses. Simply stated, Annie Mahoney-Maxwell and Joy Fiancetti are once again in peril." Fred lets that point hit home before continuing. He sees that it's made its mark by the looks on the faces of the RFI team and their loved ones. "As of this moment The Compound is locked down. Annie, you are back at the Computer Center with Joy whenever she requests. Rocco will be working alongside the two of you unless he is called to the field. Randy will be working remotely. His first assignment is a deep dive on the FBI Agents handling Manuel's care."

Fred addresses Dr. Weinstock, "I discussed this issue with Director Webber and she is in agreement that RFI needs to check into your team members' backgrounds since you will be inside the fortress when many of our team members are gone."

The doctor nods, "I would expect nothing less from RFI, Detective Serpico."

"One other thing, Doctor. When you and your agents are cleared, you will be working at the direction of RFI. You will be armed and expected to offer protection to this Compound. Director Webber will accept your phone call for confirmation of these orders. Do you have any questions at this time, Special Agent Weinstock?"

"I do not. Am I permitted to return to my patient?"

Fred nods. The doctor approaches and offers his hand before leaving the great room, "My team will come up clean, and we will provide safety measures here while you are working the Leavy case. Good luck, Fred."

The detective gathers his thoughts as the doctor returns to Manuel. "Okay, next up, Steve is in control of security. He will be giving you specifics during regularly planned sessions and protocol updates whenever there is a change in status regarding personnel at The Compound. All trained personnel will be armed 24/7. Steve will be addressing you after this meeting. There are small children at The Compound. I know I don't have to address safety measures, but let's be mindful of visuals. Pick a place for your piece, then cover it. Use a sweatshirt for a shoulder holster, jeans for an ankle holster. This is a heavily armed fortress, but it's also a home to small children.

"Update on Callie and Tess. They've been visiting David Cluster and Jane Harper since the Remington shooting and will continue their stay in Mayflower-Laurel Falls. Cluster and his team will offer 24-7 protection to the girls until further notice. If a call comes from Sergeant Cluster or his partner Sergeant Spiel, transfer the call to Rocco or Steve." Fred finds his woman's eyes and throws her a wink and a smile. "That's it for me. If anyone wants the floor or has questions, now's the time because Mike and I are gonna roll in five."

The group quietly disbands leaving Kitt and Fred and Annie and Mike to their goodbyes. Silent promises of the men's return are sealed with a kiss or two, or three, or…

Twisted little ditty.

Layne Osterman receives her next mission from her handler, "Go to Drexel Hill, Pennsylvania. Get rid of Penny Meehan. She's managed to escape death twice, Layne, so work an attack plan. She's ex-military and needs to be thought of as an enemy combatant. The stakes are high—she may not know it, but she found stuff when she was snooping in DC. The other target is the Philly detective, Ted Brothers. He was on Old Estate Road the night Boston killed Stacy Remington. You take him out, the rest of them will know for sure they are on an elimination list. They'll pull back on their advancement." The handler disconnects.

The Realm sniper does a little computer work before heading to the firing range. "Staff Sergeant Penelope Meehan, Army Reserves. Philly PD Detective Theodore Brothers. Drexel Hill, a neighborhood in the township of Upper Darby … eight miles from the center of Philly. Brothers' residence, a modified log cabin on Lower Creek Road. Sounds nice. Might be hard to sell after the upcoming double murder." She laughs. The sniper spends a couple of hours becoming one with her rifle then heads back to Sarge's place, grabs some grub, grabs a nap, then grabs her gear and tosses it into the cherry red Camaro she confiscated from the very dead Benton Brettenvue. She gets into a familiar back and forth with her host, "Sarge, I may need a place to go low for a while."

"You found my place once, you can find it again. Good luck, Ranger. Don't forget to make the call before the shot—"

"Geronimo," they yell in unison.

Layne Osterman is on the road before sunset and driving by the detective's modified log cabin in Drexel Hill by early evening. She's been given two weeks to accomplish the job. "Taking out a cop is no easy feat and so far, luck has been on the reporter's side. Luck is about to change." The amped up sniper swings around at the end of Brothers' street and takes another cruise by the cop's place. As she does, she sings a twisted little ditty, "Find a Penny, shoot the fuck, all day long, you'll have good luck." Layne lets out a l.o.n.g. laugh. "Can't wait to tell the handler that one."

Philadelphia Officer, Landry, pulls his cruiser onto Ted Brothers' driveway. As he does, he eyes the tail end of a sweet cherry red Camaro making its way down Lower Creek. Os, as he's referred to by friends, none of whom know his first name because none has ever asked, lets out a long whistle at the rolling beauty, then rushes to the detective's door hoping to beat the frigid air from taking hold. He knocks, knocks again, then rings the bell. He is just about to leave when the detective answers the door.

"Landry, come on in. What brings you by?"

"Straight up, Detective, the scratching sound Ms. Meehan heard the night of Mason Trellis' shooting didn't come from him trying to get into the house. He was trying to get into the garage. The forensic team looked seven ways to Sunday for fresh scratch marks on the house lock. There were none. Plenty on the garage door, though. Internal Affairs is going to put you on indefinite leave, sir—but you didn't hear that from me, sir. The shoot is clean, but there's some pushback from DC, so IA is gonna spend some extra time."

Ted hasn't said a word. The young officer begins feeling the heat, "Well, I'd better be going."

Ted slaps Landry's shoulder, "Thanks for the heads up, Os. Be safe out there."

"Yes, sir."

Ted makes a call to Fred, "I have a problem."

Fred laughs, "Good, cause I'm fresh out of problems today. So, lay it on me, Theodore."

"Trellis wasn't trying to get into the log cabin, he was trying to get into the garage to get his hands on the files I picked up from the Carriage House. Trellis must have been at Granger's that night. The timing sure plays out. He probably came through the woods like Boston, saw Penny and me at the Carriage House and trekked back out. That puts his arrival in Drexel Hill around the time we did lights out. Penny and I came directly home after getting the files, we spent some time together, then hit the recliners. It was maybe an hour later that Penny heard the scratching sounds. At the time we thought Trellis was trying to get into the house to hit Penny. I still think that was part of his plan, but he wanted those files, first. Officer Landry came by earlier and said Internal Affairs is putting me on leave, said there's pushback from DC. Looks like I'm out of a job and at your disposal for the foreseeable future."

Fred laughs again, "Sorry, Ted, but I'm not seeing the problem, here."

275 Market Street
The owners of the converted factory building, Malcolm Price and Gretchen Mitchell, are hosting their friends, Fred Serpico, Mike Monopoli, The Kid, and The Justice. The RFI

detectives moved into an apartment on the seventh floor then headed upstairs to hang out.

Fred fills the group in on Ted Brothers' call, then shares his thoughts, "Ted's timeout from the Philly PD is good for us. Brothers is a brilliant detective, but it's his Poindexter mathematician skillset that makes things fun. And he's a package deal now; he comes with a highly skilled investigative reporter. I don't think I ever told you guys that Penny Meehan found a notation in Granger Mitchell's files that lit some shit up for us. Granger recorded that Celia Brettenvue said The Realm is full of doctors, lawyers, and Indian chiefs. Penny wrote it off as an ethnic slur, but circled back around and connected Indian chief to Geronimo, which is the paratrooper call of Army rangers. That piece of the puzzle connected us to Eli Reynolds as the doctor and Mathis Reynolds as the lawyer. Unfortunately, that connection was made simultaneously with Manuel's shooting and Leavy's kidnapping."

Fred pauses. He fills that time with a long pull of Sam Adams and a warning, "There'd better be pepperoni pizza for me when I'm done talking."

He receives a collective, "Mmmmm," from the group.

"Okay, back at it. Malcolm and Gretchen, how are you guys with Penny? Are there residuals about her association with Abigail? Before you answer, I'd like to say that she's left the dark side of tabloid reporting and has become an invaluable team member. If Ted joins us here, she joins us here. This is your place, so if that arrangement isn't—"

Malcolm interrupts the detective, "Fred. Penny is welcome here."

"Don't like interruptions, Mr. Mayor."

"Don't care, Fred."

"Okay, then. Next topic. Mike check with Rocco on the legalities of a benched detective working with us. I know we can use him on investigative work, but I need to know if he's covered for field work, particularly weapon's related field work. Randy, you'll be working here, but you will report to Joy and Rocco. Annie is going back into the Computer Center. Initially, she's going to be working on a new signature, whatever the hell that is, but will be a resource to the cyber team. Malcolm and Gretchen, the apartments on the seventh floor are perfect. Most of our investigative and research work will be done down there. When we need to be on the eighth floor we'll limit our work to the Diving Center. Lastly, Peyton Wells, the head of Rocco Fiancetti Incorporated plans to speak to you about a consultant position as soon as the dust settles—so no time soon." He laughs big. "I've been authorized to put you on a retainer of $50,000. Your skillset is research, so we will pair you with Penny." Fred claps his hands once, "Okay, I'm done. I need a pepperoni pizza and a few beers."

Gretchen hands him a box.

He growls. "One slice? Who ate…"

Gretchen smiles and pats her baby ball then reaches for a second box near her feet, "Here. This one's for you."

"Thank you, Gretchen."

"You're welcome, Fred."

The Compound

Joy and Rocco Fiancetti have been diving for hours looking for any sign of Leavy or chatter about her kidnapping. "No sign of her signature, and there's absolutely nothing in cyberland that indicates anyone knows about her predicament."

"Si, Gia, and the news media is still in the dark. That means the only other people who know Leavy has been kidnapped are the ones who took her."

Annie has been working quietly alongside her bosses on her new cyber signature. It's been nearly a year since she has put any measurable time in at the Center, though her keystrokes suggest there's been no time away. When the #2 ranked cyber huntress has completed the task of signature creation, she takes it for a deep dive for Joy's review.

"Nice, Annie. It's far enough from your original signature that no one will suspect the Girl Genius is back in the deep—until they see your speed, that is—but they'll never be able to catch up to you, so it's all good. Now, I'd like you to create an equally difficult spare signature. You, too, Rocco."

The two hunters each raise a brow.

The director of the Computer Center explains, "It's something I instituted when John and Leavy came onboard. I mandated that each of us develop a spare signature in case any of us were ever taken. Rocco, on your recent dives you've been looking for Leavy's original signature. I've been looking for her spare. Her captors will know her original signature. When they are ready to use her, they will make her create a new one before allowing her into cyberland. When that happens, she is going to create the one she already has on file here. That way when they allow her back into cyberland we will be alerted. We will follow her, and we will find her. John knows Leavy's spare signature. I'm sure he's already looking for it. As soon as you two are back in, we'll have four of us looking for it."

Rocco wheels away from his station and goes to his wife, "Mi amore, you are preeminent in every way possible," he says with a kiss. "I will go see my son and be back to create my spare."

Snowfall Prison

Hannah Leavy wills her eyes open even though they'll reveal her new world. Her accommodations are quite lovely and very comfortable, but they are a prison, and she is a hostage of a nefarious crime organization.

The instant she stirs, her captor speaks, "Leavy, you've been asleep for ten hours. You need to get up and move around, clean up, and have something to eat."

Leavy pushes herself to a sitting position, swings her legs to the floor and waits for him to approach her. He tosses a key onto her bed, "You know the drill. Unlock your chains, leave the short chain on, leave the key on the bed, wait for my direction, then stand. Don't do anything stupid, Leavy, I will shoot you. Understood?"

"Understood."

The prisoner has permission to close the bathroom door when she relieves herself, showers, and dresses. When she is finished with her morning routine she asks, "May I exit?"

"Yes, take your seat at the table."

She does at she is told.

Once seated, Eli slides the key toward her. She takes it, affixes the table chains to her short chain and locks them together. She then places the key onto the table.

Her captor walks from across the room, retrieves the key and inspects the chains. "I made scrambled eggs and toast this morning. Orange or grapefruit juice?"

"Either."

"Choose one, Leavy. I want you to adapt to your new life and participate in it. You are here against your will, but you are with me. Objectionable as that may seem now, you will come to realize this existence is far better than being in a Peruvian cell under the thumb of a ruthless crime lord. You are best to remember that."

Leavy nods, "Orange juice, please. May I ask a question?"

"In a moment. Place your hands under your ass while I put your food on the table. Don't move a muscle." Eli leaves a plastic plate, utensils, and juice cup on the table within reach of Leavy and steps away. "You may ask your question."

"I have not touched a keyboard since my arrival, yet you took me for my cyber skills. Is that correct?"

"Partly," Eli answers flatly.

Goosebumps run her arms. She chooses to ignore them and the not so subtle meaning behind Eli's word. "When will I begin work for your organization?"

"When we have the other pieces in place. Until then you will not be allowed anywhere near a computer. For the foreseeable future, Leavy, you will be expected to accept your new life, acclimate to your surroundings, and adhere to the rules set for you."

Leavy nods through sudden tears that spring.

"What are the rules, Leavy?"

"Don't try to escape. Don't try to engage with others. Don't ask about Manuel."

Working his way back.

Rocco pulls a chair next to Manuel's bed. He places his hand onto his son's leg and begins the mind-numbing back and forth movement of his thumb, the only touch that can connect them. Within seconds he is lost to the past…

Genoa, Italy
1989

Rocco exited the Fiancetti heat studio needing relief from the sweltering box. Sweat droplets rolled down his face and chest and onto the steamy brick inlay at his feet. The bib of his jean overalls hung at his waist, caked with that day's sweat and dust. Sinewy, exaggerated muscles ran his arms, having been raised from the brute work at the kiln. The overheated man pulled a long breath, but found no relief in the stifling, stagnant air. The handkerchief he pulled from his back pocket drenched quickly as he wiped his face and neck.

"You work a kiln?"

Rocco turned quickly and found the keeper of the voice, an exquisite wonder standing at the end of the brick alleyway. "Si."

"Continuous or intermittent?" the chestnut haired, sienna eyed, olive skinned beauty asked.

"Continuous," Rocco said as he walked toward her. "How do you know about kilns?"

"Picked up a little information here and there. What type of work do you do?"

"My current project is a series of ceramic tiles for a mosaic installation at the gallery."

"The Fiancetti Gallery?" she asked with enthusiasm.

Rocco nodded.

"It is a beautiful space. I just spent two hours there. Lorenzo Fiancetti is ..... well, you know how brilliant he is."

"How so?"

"You are working in his studio, and you said you will be doing an installation at his gallery. You must recognize his talent, and he yours," she smiled.

Rocco studied the young woman. His attention unnerved her. "I apologize for staring, but you are quite exquisite. You are Greek, si?"

"I should be going. It's getting late. Good luck with your installation."

Before he could respond, the wonder was gone.

~

Rocco spent a few minutes at the closed Fiancetti Gallery surveying his completed pieces. The image was taking shape as the mosaics lined up and touched one another.

Rocco was joined in the private room by his father, world renowned artist Lorenzo Fiancetti.

"It is quite beautiful, son. Was your day at the kiln successful?"

"Si. And you? Did you work at your studio?"

"No. I spent the day at the fountain at Piazza de Ferrari with my sketch pad. Perhaps tomorrow I will lock myself in the studio. How long before you are ready to install your piece?"

"Two days at the kiln three days to install. Do you think I made an error using only three colors?"

"That is a question only you can answer. It was a risk. A bold risk. You fear people will think I created it and question whether it is your work, si?"

Rocco nodded.

The father tapped his son's shoulder, "Go home. Get some rest. Finish your piece and let the world have their say. You are an artist, Rocco. The need to create will fuel you. Self-doubt will chase you. Welcome to the club."

~

Rocco left out the back door of the gallery, made his way to the studio to check the kiln, then moved down the brick alleyway toward his terraced apartment. As he passed a doorway, he found the exquisite wonder crouched tight in the small space, her knees pulled to her chest, her face pressed deep against them.

"What the hell do you think you're doing?" Rocco demanded.

Wonder began to rise, "I'm sorry. I'll find another place."

"You'll come with me."

She flinched—made a move to get around him.

"Don't even think about running. What's your name?"

"I'd rather not say."

"What do you want me to call you?"

"You pick," she said with a shrug.

Rocco scoffed, "You'll tell me when you're ready. I'm Rocco. Let's go."

"Where?"

"My place."

She stopped.

He stopped.

"I have a garden flat. I'll leave the terrace doors open and will not try to stop you from leaving. You look as though you haven't eaten or rested in days."

Her exhale seemed to take with it the last bit of energy she had. The silent wonder didn't pull away when he took hold of her hand and led her into his garden place.

"Do you want food or a nap first?"

"Could I take a shower, please?"

"It's right through there. Whatever you need is in the closet in the bathroom or in the bedroom chest of drawers."

Twenty minutes later Wonder emerged with her hair wrapped in a towel and her face scrubbed clean. She had on a pair of jeans and one of Rocco's T-shirts, "I hope you don't mind. I needed to rinse my shirts and you said to take what I needed."

He eyed the exceedingly beautiful young woman, couldn't help but notice her rounded breasts and pebbled nipples, "My T-shirt never looked better."

She neither responded nor shied from his attention.

"I have reheated lasagna," the host said as he placed her plate on the table. He poured her a glass of wine then sat opposite her. "How long have you been on the streets?"

Wonder, with the sienna eyes, finished her mouthful and smiled, "It's not like that. I have a home. I prefer not to be in it."

"Is someone after you?"

She took another bite and nodded.

"Has someone hurt you?" Rocco watched her face, her beautiful face. Her eyes glistened with tears that held tight. "I think I should go. My things can dry outside, and I can return your shirt tomorrow." She pushed her chair back and got up.

He did the same. "I think you should stay the night. If you sit and finish your meal. I won't ask any questions."

Before she sat, she unwrapped her hair, shook the long chestnut waves free, and pulled the front section to one side. She waited for

Rocco to sit before she began eating again,
"This is very delicious. Thank you for sharing."

"Thank you for staying. Otherwise I would have
had to follow you throughout the labyrinth streets of
Genoa. It would have made for a very long night."

Rocco is pulled from his memories by a
twitch in Manuel's leg. The father remains
deathly still hoping for another sign. None
comes, but Rocco leaves his son's bedside
knowing Manuel is working his way back.

Surveillance and secret meetings.

Layne Osterman decides the Camaro needs to go; it draws way too much attention. The problem is she boosted it from a dead guy, and he probably boosted it from some other guy. She gives Sergeant Noone a call. "I should have asked this question when I was with you, Sarge, but any chance I can switch the Camaro for one of your rides?"

"Meet me half-way. I'll leave in twenty minutes. Just pull to the side of the road. I'll find that cherry red piece of yours."

"Thanks, Sarge."

Before heading to the meet-up, Layne drives past Ted Brothers' place. She sees the Land Rover on the driveway, "That's been there since I first came by." She also spies a blue Honda Civic parked behind it, "but that's new." She slows her roll, swings around, drives back, and reads the magnetized business sign on the car's front door.

Drexel Hill Physical Therapy
When You Can't Come to Us
We'll Come to You

The Realm contract killer checks the time, 10:30 AM. "No way I'll make it back before the therapy session ends." She leaves Drexel Hill, gets onto the highway and opens up the Camaro. A mile or so into the trip she begins her little ditty and turns it into a mantra, "Find a Penny, shoot the fuck, all day long, you'll have good luck."

Somewhere in DC
At the insistence of imprisoned Paul Ferraro, aka Boston, Felicity Ferraro, aka The Face, called an emergency meeting with the Gang of Eight. When she arrives, fashionably late, the ancillary leaders are sufficiently torqued. As usual Jack McGovern is the one who gets all up in Felicity's face.

"Where the fuck is Turner? Who gave the order to take out Rocco Fiancetti's son? Is there an elimination list? What the fuck is going on?"

"Sit down. All of you." When their asses find seats and the anger-fueled dust settles a bit, she joins them at the table. "Senator Rodgers is where he needs to be, and he's doing what he said he'd be doing—concentrating on his campaign and getting to the Oval Office. As for who gave the order to take out Manuel Xavier and whether there is an elimination list, you know damned well who gave the order, and you know damned well there is a list. Until such time as every person present at the Stacy Remington assassination is eliminated, there will be a rash of sudden deaths. I do not expect to be notified by any of you when breaking news reports are announced. As to what the fuck is going on, we are in the long game, ladies and gentlemen. From Day One, The Body has been in charge. There is no change there. From Day One, each of you chose to be passive observers, until such time as your expertise is required. There is no change in that regard. You have not been consulted on strategy or execution in the past, nor will you be consulted now. You are witnesses. Your leadership roles are based on ancillary contributions you make to the organization, not for your input on day to day or long-range planning. You have been protected by operatives who are actually doing the grunt work—those who are now paying the price."

She drills them with a lengthy stare. "Roland Gaffney is sitting in a Federal prison, and though he could destroy every one of us, he has not said a single word about The Realm or the people in the organization. Under tremendous duress and to the detriment of herself, Dominique Brettenvue gave up Tango leaders when she easily could have presented this lot to the authorities. Paul Ferraro is bearing it out in prison waiting to learn his fate—and **you**," she scoffs, "you come to this meeting with questions and demands. Your willing acceptance as pawns on the playing board confirms that you deserve no answers to your questions or settlement of your demands."

The Face gets up and walks the perimeter of the room before sitting again, "I am the conduit between the leader of this organization and the Gang. The message from our boss is this: The Realm is at a critical juncture. Once The Body has put important pieces in place, you will be invited into the decision-making process. I have been told to pass on a directive: stay calm, put your noses down, and be patient. As for you, Jack, get your ass into the Bureau and get us information. You sit between Director Shelby Webber and FICA Director John Maxwell. Find out what they know or what they think they know. Shit is happening all around them, Jack. They are smart enough to know there is an elimination going on. They are putting their heads together and are most likely working with RFI. Find out what their plans are and report back."

Jack begins to fume. "Here's my report back, Felicity. The two directors spent the past couple days at Webber's waterfront place working the case, or working each other. I haven't a clue, but as long as they are working from there, we don't have eyes and ears."

"Find a way to get what we need. The rest of you stay out of my way." Felicity notices a look between two Gang members. She makes a mental note to discuss the powerful duo with Paul.

After the Gang of Eight leaves, The Face sits alone in the barely lit conference room. The empty seats around the table drive home a bitter truth—she is truly alone in this fucking mess. Her thoughts drift from the current state of things to the family life she enjoyed just a month ago…

The mother ushered her brood from the garage to the kitchen as singsong calls of, "Daddy's home!" rang out.

Boston was pulled from his upstairs office by the sounds of his family returning home. He ran downstairs arriving just as his troops began storming the kitchen. He moved backward in exaggerated form, absorbing the rush of little bodies and flying limbs. "Let's see how many there are today: one, two, three, four." Boston touched each child's head, smiled at his kids, then headed to his wife, Felicity, who was bringing up the rear. "Hey, babe," he smiled wide. "I've missed the hell out of you. Let's get the troops to bed early and do a little dancing."

The wife's smile dazzled at her husband's suggestion—dancing was, after all, their code for sexual ravaging. "You know I love to dance,

Paul. Should I be warming up for any particular sway this evening?" she asked in her lilting brogue.

His smile cut long, deep dimples as he ran his hooded lustful eyes over his mahogany-haired, blue-eyed, fair-skinned, Irish lass. "The Tango, of course."

The Realm associate known as "Irish" nodded and smiled at her man, "There's no dance quite like the Tango."

...then to the day she left her children with nothing more than a kiss goodbye...

Felicity Ferraro spent a restless night banging up against the little elbows, knees, and feet of her brood. She pulled the last of her little ones from her king-size bed with an excited, "Come on. Come on. You need to finish packing. Mommy is way ahead of you slack-abouts," she pulled her stuffed suitcase from the floor, flopped it onto the bed with a "Whoomph," to the delighted squeal of her children.

On the way to the airport, the mother joined her kids in song, regaled them with the things they would do on vacation, and handed them crackers and drinks, "Nibble and sip quickly. You can't bring those onto the plane." An hour later, Felicity pulled her SUV to a curb, placed a kiss on the forehead of each of her unconscious children, released them without word to the custody of a family member, then waited until the plane lifted off. She drove from the airport in tears.

...then to the day she learned her imprisoned husband double-crossed her...

Attorney Ferraro was already seated when her husband was brought into the meeting room. She waited through the unshackling, the seating, and the re-shackling before speaking.

"I think…"

"Don't say a fucking word, Felicity."

She crossed her arms and leaned back.

"I heard that you got a promotion. I heard that you've bought yourself some time with the Gang of Eight. I heard that you've sent our children away."

"How?"

"Shut. The. Fuck. Up."

Felicity remained deathly still.

"Where are our children, Felicity?"

"With my family in Dublin."

Paul shook his head. "Nope." Paul smiled wide. "**My** children are not on their way to Dublin."

"What have you done?"

"I took what's mine."

"Paul…"

"Shut the fuck up. You need to be put in your place, Felicity. You made a unilateral decision for our children. You need to be punished for that. You **think** you are calling the shots—with me, with our kids, hell, you **think** you are The Face of an international crime organization." **He let out a maniacal laugh.** "You **think** you were hand-selected by The Body. You don't even know who The Body is."

"What?"

"Turner Rodgers is not The Body." Paul remained silent for several minutes. He enjoyed the multitude of changes that crossed his wife's face, her beautiful albeit strained face.

"Who is The Body?"

"The Body is every single person you encounter, so watch your step and your mouth, wifey." **He gave her another minute then said,** "Get your ass over here, give your husband a kiss and lift your skirt."

Felicity looked at the door, "I can't, it's against the rules."

"**I** fucking make the rules, Felicity. Now, wrap your pussy around my dick."

The woman caught in deep, painful reflection is pulled from her thoughts by her ringing cell. She scans the still empty conference room. "Felicity Ferraro," she answers.

"Mrs. Ferraro, this is Mathis Reynolds. I believe you've heard of me. I am The Body."

Weddings and warnings.

Randy completes his deep dive into Manuel's FBI medical team: Special Agent Gregory Weinstock, FBI Agent Candace Hayes, and FBI Agent Chase Jones. Despite their clean records, there is a little something to tell Naught-Naught-Zero.

"Fiancetti," Rocco answers immediately.

"Yo, Naught-Naught."

The ridiculous reference brings a much-needed chuckle to the head of RFI, "I presume you have completed your dives on Manuel's medical team. Inform, please."

"All three agents pass inspection, sir. However two of them are secret-keepers. Dr. Weinstock and Physician's Assistant Hayes are husband and wife. Their weddedness is brandy-new."

"Explain."

"Weinstock and Hayes have been colleagues for two years and down-low romanticizers for a year or so. They spent a wedding week at the Boca Raton home of Sam and Pam Peterson, relatives of the bride, and were back in DC a handful of hours when they were dispatched to handle Manuel's shooting."

"Any indication that Director Webber is aware of this union?"

"Unsure, but marital paperwork has not been filed at FBI Headquarters."

"Assessment, Randall?"

"I think it's nothing more than timing, sir. You'll get a better sense when you interrogate the newlyweds. And when you're done with the waterboarding, ask them where they're registered. The Kid wants to send them a little something."

"Thank you for the update. Please connect with Joy for your next assignment."

"Call the woman who's knotted with the Naught-Naught. I'm on it, sir."

Rocco holds his laughter until the call is ended.

Dr. Gregory Weinstock analyzes Rocco Fiancetti's body language as he approaches the medical staff. The doctor taps the shoulder of Physician's Assistant Candace Hayes and motions his head for her to follow him. They leave Manuel's care to Maura.

"Explain," Rocco directs.

"Timing. We got the call from J. Edgar that our services were needed hours after we returned to DC from Florida. It's been balls to the wall since we arrived at MedStar and ended up here. We haven't gone through FBI protocol for married agents, and when we do we will be separated. Mr. Fiancetti, Manuel cannot afford for us to be separated. My three-person medical team is the best at the Bureau. There will be consequences for our choice to ignore protocol, which we will accept. What we cannot accept is being removed from his case."

The head of RFI likes what he just heard. "Very well, Dr. Weinstock. I will be discussing this matter with Director Webber. Put aside your concerns. You will continue caring for my son until such time as he does not require your team. Then you will deal with the FBI brass." Rocco looks toward Manuel's room, "I will make a call to Director Webber then return."

Alexandria
Shelby Webber cuts to the chase with Rocco, "I'm in agreement that the medical team remains at RFI. The agents have impeccable records and stellar medical expertise which negates any issues regarding paperwork protocol. A change of subject, Rocco. Now that we have Mathis and Eli Reynolds in our sights and a building suspicion that Deputy Director Jack McGovern is in The Realm, we have several significant threads to pull. I will be meeting with FICA

Director Maxwell later in the day to start pulling them."

"An observation of Maxwell, if you will permit."

"Proceed."

"There is no one in the world better at cyber defense than John Maxwell. That fact tends to overshadow his highly effective and unusual investigative skillset. Traditional investigators, I include myself in this group, look for the reasons why something happened. John first looks for reasons why other things did not happen. His ruminations eventually circle back to the traditionalist's way of processing, but along the way he finds very useful case elements. I mention this because a situation might arise when you will want him to follow **your** instincts, when you want to reign him in. My experience suggests John Maxwell needs free reign, Director. That's when he's at his best."

Loves – past and present.

Rocco sits at his son's bedside and connects with him in the only permissible way. The father's touch upon his boy's leg brings comfort when only days before it brought despair. In a few moments' time the quiet man is once again lost to his thoughts…

Genoa, Italy
1989

"My name is Eleni Karras. I am the only child of Greek shipping tycoon, Andros Karras. Depending on your point of view, I am on an unplanned holiday traveling across Europe… or I have run away from my father's home on the island of Santorini."

"Are you traveling alone? Completely alone?"

"But of course. It is customary that runaways embark on a solitary journey, si?"

"Perhaps. But most runaways aren't as beautiful as you, Eleni. You are asking for trouble being on your own."

"Most of my days on Earth have included trouble, Rocco. I have just begun my travels, and have several more cities and many more galleries to find. If you don't want my travels to be lonely, come with," she tossed a playful smile his way.

Rocco said nothing for a few minutes. "I need five days to finish the installation at the gallery. If you stay here with me during that time, I will travel with you."

Eleni clapped her hands and ran to Rocco. She wrapped her arms around his neck and pecked him on his cheek. "We will have romance and adventure. A summer to remember."

~

The evening of the private unveiling of Rocco's mosaic began with excitement and ended with enticement.

"It is exquisite Rocco," Eleni said for the umpteenth time.

Rocco swelled with pride, "I have been questioning the choice of three colors."

Eleni's eyes did not leave his work, "...because of your father's success with tri-color work?"

"Si."

Eleni took hold of the young artist's hand, "This work is uniquely your own, Rocco. I think it is bold to enter his world and find your own place within. I fancy myself a devotee of your father's work, so believe me when I say that this piece will usher you toward your own place in the art world."

"Eleni is correct, son," Lorenzo spoke from behind them. "This work is a triumph. The choice of blue, brown, and white, and the placement of the tiles is perfection. The final piece demands attention. The power, the serenity, the wonder, it's all there."

"It's Santorini," Eleni whispered.

"What?" the men asked.

"The mosaic. It's Santorini. The colors are of my homeland. The brown represents the carved out, assaulted terrain left behind after one of Earth's most powerful volcanos ever to be recorded. The white swaths across the top of the earth tones represents the whitewash houses perched precariously over a land destined to roar again. And the blues of the sky and the sea seem to share a clandestine kiss on the horizon that locks the story of Santorini."

Rocco released Eleni's hand and placed his on either side of her face. He ran his thumbs over every inch of her beauty, then pulled her in for a claiming kiss. His desire captured every bit of air from the room. The soon-to-be-lovers barely heard the closing of the door behind Lorenzo.

"Eleni." Rocco touched and kissed the wonder who walked into his life only days before. He had yet to enter her, but her silk was already home to him. He celebrated her beauty with feather soft kisses and owning touches as he stripped her bare. His response was fierce, his touch, reverent. "Exquisite. You are a work of art."

Eleni pressed herself tight against him, touched his face and with shaking hands began undressing him. Her moves were halting, her breathing hitched with desire… uncertainty.

Rocco shared his nakedness, his want powerfully displayed.

Eleni raised a hand to her cheek to conceal the blush that took hold.

Rocco feared the signs, "Eleni, am I the first?"

Tears stung her eyes, "Yes."

He stepped back.

She closed the space between them. "Rocco, I have never given myself to anyone. I have never desired this. I have never trusted anyone. Please let me have this with you beneath your beautiful masterpiece." Silent tears fell from beneath closed lashes, as she felt him walk away. Her pain and embarrassment began to settle, yet she was unable to move, unable to cover her naked pain.

A touch on her arms startled her. "Come, Eleni." Rocco directed her to the bed he'd made of their clothes and set beneath his mosaic. They lay together, touching, kissing, offering themselves. He waited until she was ready. His probing was gentle, her response unbridled. When she begged him to enter her, he begged her to never leave.

Eleni's release was quick and steady.

Rocco's was halted. He abruptly pulled himself free and moaned against her as he finished, "Eleni. Eleni." He looked at the beauty beneath him. "Eleni, look at me."

Her focus was fleeting, her smile, telling. "Rocco. Such wonders of life. Thank you." She reached to touch his face.

He took her hand and kissed its palm. "Eleni, are you on the pill or anything?"

The young woman, who had part of her lover pooled within, pushed from beneath him. "I have to go," she said on a panic.

"Go? You aren't going anywhere, Eleni." He tried to pull her to him.

She pushed angrily away. "I have to go, Rocco. He will kill you if he learns of this." Her panic swelled as she hurriedly donned her clothes.

Rocco responded in kind, pushing his legs into his jeans. "Eleni, tell me what is going on. Are you having regrets about us?"

She shook her head, "No regrets of us. But I have put you in danger. I am the daughter of a ruthless man. He does not see me as your father sees you, Rocco. To Andros Karras, I am a possession, his prized possession. If he learns that you have defiled and perhaps impregnated his prized possession, he will destroy you."

Rocco pulled his wonder to him. "If another man tries to take you away, I will destroy him."

The touch of Joy's hand on Rocco's arm pulls him from his thoughts. "Mi amore," he says, as he pulls her onto his lap, "I was in thought."

"Yes." Joy places a hand onto each of Rocco's cheeks and looks deeply into his eyes, "It is long overdue that you surrender to the thoughts you have struggled to bury, Rocco."

As though in agreement with Joy's words, Manuel moans.

Welcome back.

There is a sudden flurry of activity at Manuel's bedside. Rocco and Joy are ushered out by Maura who fills them in on what's happening. "Manuel is pushing through. The team will reduce his meds and monitor him. Why don't you come back in a couple of hours?" Maura expects pushback, but receives none.

Manuel Xavier opens one of his eyes at the touch of his leg. The corner of his lip curls ever so slightly and a single tear falls and slides down his cheek. He tries to speak, but his word catches in his throat. Still, Rocco knows his boy said, "Papa."

Rocco stands next to his son and places his palm to Manuel's head. He runs his thumb across dark, wavy, chestnut hair, the perfect combination of his parents' locks. "My son, welcome back. I have missed your company." Rocco sees strain, and then the panic that claims Manuel's eyes. His heart picks up speed as he tries to say her name. The medical team rushes in.

"What happened?" Dr. Weinstock asks.

"He's trying to ask about Leavy." An injection is pushed into the patient's IV. His heart rate slows, his eyes hood and then close. The emergency has passed.

"Agents Hayes and Jones please stay with the patient. Everyone else, out. The patient cannot handle any news about Leavy. It is imperative that he recovers memories on his own and incrementally. His asking for her means he already senses her absence. He's eventually going to get to the memory of being shot and what that means for his team member."

"His woman," Rocco interjects. "Hannah Leavy is far more than his team member. The two have been in a prolonged state of unexpressed love until very recently. If Manuel does not see Leavy at his bedside he will know it is because she is hurt, she is dead, or she has been kidnapped. So, doctor, what is our plan?"

"He has been through a great deal today and is going to experience his own level of exhaustion and succumb to it. We will assist with his inertia when warranted. In the meantime, Maura and Rocco you two are out of his room. He is less likely to ask the rest of us about Hannah Leavy because he will assume his doctor and nurses don't know anything. We will give you updates, and you can sit at the monitors. Until further notice, that is the extent of your access to my patient. Now, if you will excuse me."

275

Fred receives a call from a relieved Rocco, then places a call to John Maxwell's cell phone. He doesn't expect John to answer the call. It is hours before Fred hears back.

"I was starting to worry, John," Fred teases.

"I'm just heading to the hotel. What's up?"

"Is this line secure?"

"It's a single use burner. What's up?" John asks again.

"Manuel is awake."

John can feel Fred's smile and adds one of his own, "That's damned good news, Fred. Step one."

"Yeah, but he asked about Leavy? We have to find her."

"We will. Hang on Fred, I'm getting into the elevator at the hotel."

Fred waits, and waits a bit more, then hears the ding indicating John is at his floor.

"Anything else before I … oh, for fuck's sake. My place has been tossed. I've gotta go."

Shelby Webber reluctantly takes John Maxwell's call. "Can this wait Director Maxwell?"

"Just letting you know I've called a couple forensic guys to my hotel room. It's been tossed. Nothing is missing, but I found three listening devices where there were no listening devices this morning. As soon as the team is done, I'll be checking into another hotel."

"What about your vehicle?"

"Leaving it here, ma'am. It's got a GPS trap on it. I don't want to lead my eyes and ears directly to my new place. I'll catch a ride with one of the techs."

"Contact Agent Rhys and have her handle your accommodations."

John ends the call and quickly digs through his files. He pulls the one on Agent Amanda Rhys and gives it a quick read. "A two-year employee of the FBI. She was given a desk assignment after a raid in Sherman Oaks, California, resulted in the deaths of two agents and three civilians. It was Rhys' first and last field raid. At the request of Shelby Webber, the agent was brought in from the field and put in charge of the day to day operations for the director and deputy director, and now for the director of FICA." He places the call.

"Agent Rhys," she answers on the first ring.

"This is Director Maxwell. Are you on a secure line, Agent?"

"Yes, sir."

"My hotel room was tossed and bugged. I need replacement accommodations. Make it for tonight only. I'll want to move daily until I rent a place. Director Webber needs to be informed where I'll be staying."

"Permission to speak freely, sir?"

"Yes."

"I considered calling Director Webber at home. I had a concern earlier, now I have a hinky feeling, sir."

"Explain."

"When I returned to my station at J. Edgar shortly before 3 PM today, I saw Deputy Director McGovern exiting Director Webber's office. At 6 PM I knocked on the Director's door to inform her that I was leaving for the day. There was no response. This situation has been banging in my head all evening, Director Maxwell. My concern is that Deputy Director McGovern was in Director Webber's office without her being present. Unless he received approval to be in her office unattended, he was in direct breach of protocol."

"Agent Rhys, I will handle my own hotel accommodations, and I will place a call to the Director. Goodnight, Agent."

John places a second call to his boss.

"How can I be of assistance, Director Maxwell."

"Are you on a secure line, Director?"

"Yes."

"No ma'am, you are not."

We might get lucky with the trap.

Tiny pebbles hit her window. She looks out over a dark backyard and sees the tiny flash of a pen light. "John Maxwell," she whisper-groans. "He breached security. Again. This time, he took out the damned floodlights." She heads to the lower level and opens the door for him. He is near-frozen despite his wearing a Navy pea coat, a black wool watchman's cap, and gloves. He puts his finger to his lips, follows her to the house, and softly drops a black backpack just inside the door. He slips past the wondering woman, heads to the kitchen and slides open a drawer in which he noticed paper and a pen when he was rummaging for coffee days before. He writes his message. **Rhys saw McGovern leave your office while you weren't there. I think you brought ears home. Let's talk upstairs.**

As soon as they are behind closed doors, John starts in, "Were you in your office this afternoon between the hours of three and six?"

"No. I was out of the building."

"Rhys thought you were behind closed doors. Why was she unaware that you were gone?"

"I had an urgent matter that needed immediate attention. I neglected to inform Agent

Rhys of my whereabouts."

"Director Webber, your deputy director broke protocol by entering your office when it was unattended. His exit was witnessed by Agent Rhys. There is a reason he broke protocol. Did you tell him you were handling an urgent matter outside of J. Edgar?"

"No."

John nods. "Ma'am I suspect your office is bugged and you have subsequently brought home a listening device or two. We need to check everything you carried home with you today. The bug is most likely going to be in something you take back and forth, like your briefcase or purse."

"I had my purse with me off-site. We need to check my briefcases. I carry two. How do you want to proceed, John?"

"Director Maxwell," he smirks. "You should address me as Director Maxwell." He waits several seconds then throws her a smile.

"Continue, Director Maxwell." She waits several seconds then throws him a scowl.

"Yes, ma'am. If you brought home a bug, then our listener already knows that I called you tonight. He would only be privy to your end of the conversation. Even so, you asked about my vehicle and suggested I have Rhys handle new accommodations for me. Our listener knows I'm on the move. He wants me distracted—look over here at John Maxwell's bugs so I can sneak a few into Shelby Webber's house. Agent Rhys said she had a hinky feeling about McGovern being in your office and wanted to call you at home. If she had called, our listener would have heard your end of the conversation and known they were caught. I say our first step is to confirm the presence of listening devices. If we've got them, let's use them to our advantage. The thing is, you'll need to be vigilant about what you say or what you let anyone else say around your briefcase. I have a plan to trap our listener. It's something irresistible enough to put him, and maybe a few other players, in motion. We might get lucky with the trap."

Shelby thinks for several minutes, "You want to use Leavy's kidnapping to see if that revelation causes a maelstrom of activity."

John nods. "If I'm correct, and Mathis and Eli are the only Realm members who know about Leavy's kidnapping and captivity, it's going to shake the foundation of the nefarious organization."

"I agree with your assessment and your plan, but the RFI team needs to be on board. Are we clear on that point, John?"

"We are Shelby."

Novel and spare.

John Maxwell knocks on Shelby Webber's bedroom door. The Director invited him to stay the night when she learned he walked several miles to her home to handle the planted device situation. Her decency prevailed her good sense and kept her up a good portion of the night. His early morning knock makes her rethink her decision, yet again.

"What?" she clicks the lock and pulls open her door.

"Not a morning person, huh?" John smirks.

"Director Maxwell, please forgive my repetitiveness. What?"

"Pull yourself together. We have a conference call with Rocco Fiancetti and Fred Serpico at five-fifteen."

Shelby glances at her watch, "That's fifteen minutes from now," she informs the retreating Maxwell.

He calls over his shoulder, "For the record, I breached security onto your property so locking your door won't keep me out of your bedroom. Rest assured, Director, I won't step foot into your chamber until you invite me in."

Shelby slams the door.

John smirks as he bounds down the stairs.

Shelby joins John in the kitchen. The coffee is on and the table is covered with pads and pens. She raises an inquisitive brow.

"Your briefcases are outside in some sort of storage box you have by the house. I found an external bug on each. The dangling part of the main zipper has been replaced with a listening device. Do you use paperclips as a general practice?"

"Prefer butterfly clips, but others use them, so they find their way into my files. Why?"

"There's a paperclip attached to some paperwork inside a folder inside each briefcase. They are probably devices. Most people wouldn't have even noticed a paperclip being on work related materials, but they are the only ones in your bags." John places a mug of coffee with a splash of cream and a pinch of sugar in front of Shelby. "Rocco and Fred will call my cell and I'll conference you in. Don't forget, Fred hates being interrupted. We acquiesce to his ways because there is no one better than Fred Serpico. He does his processing while standing in front of a window, any window will do. He goes silent, processes his shit, then gets onto a rift that sets an investigation onto the right path.

He's brilliant." John leaps off the counter and grabs his ringing phone, "Who's on?"

"Fred."

"Rocco."

"Hang on, RFI."

"Webber, on."

It's John's dog and pony show so he begins, "Deputy Director, Jack McGovern, breached protocol yesterday by going into Director Webber's office while she was out of the building. His actions were witnessed by a reliable agent. Subsequently, I found listening devices on and in the briefcases the director carries between her home and office. We want to use those listening devices to our advantage. Test the waters on our theory that the Reynolds brothers are keeping secrets from Realm members."

"You want to use Leavy's kidnapping," Rocco and Fred unison.

"Yes. We need something, a thread, a foothold, something to help move forward our search for her. Since she's been gone, there's been no chatter in cyberland, or digging by the media, nothing to suggest anyone knows the #3 ranked cyber huntress has been kidnapped or that she's in peril. If Mathis and Eli kept this information from The Realm, let's use it to our advantage. Hey, Fred, I think I hear you hyperventilating, go ahead with your thoughts."

He jumps right in. "Let's recap. Someone bugged Stacy Remington's work office and GPS trapped her Escalade. Someone sent a death threat against Stacy to Director Webber. The director removed Stacy from the cases, which drove her investigation underground. She secretly worked from her home office on The Realm case—we know that because she analyzed the organization's structure, determined it was based on an octopus, and sent her summary work to Granger Mitchell and Manuel Xavier. We can assume she sent those notes as insurance in the event something happened to her. We know Stacy had concerns about being surveilled at home, but we don't know if she had suspicions about who her snoop was. In any event, the snoop knew she was continuing her work on The Realm and Tango. RFI pulled her into a sting operation at Granger Mitchell's house. This snoop knew she was going to be on-site and might have known her boss, the Director of the FBI, was being kept in the dark. A 20/20 review on our end suggests FICA Director Stacy Remington was the intended victim of the assassination that night. Recent events suggest there is an elimination list for those who were present at that event. I need a minute."

"Bet he's standing at a window, Rocco?"

"Si."

"See," John addresses Shelby.

"Si," Rocco responds.

"That see wasn't for you, Rocco."

"Si. I see."

"For fuck's sake," John groans.

"I'm back," Fred pushes, "did I miss anything?"

"NO!"

"Good. I have a thread that I need to pull before we move on with your Leavy plan, John."

"What's your thread?"

"Mike. I want to grill him about the time he spent at Stacy's townhouse the morning of the shooting and kidnapping. He was the last person with Manuel and Leavy, and Mathis and Eli. He was no more than a few minutes away from the townhouse when I sent him back. Within those few minutes, the Reynolds brothers either put into action a plan they'd devised, or something caused them to act in the heat of the moment. If John is right that members of The Realm are in the dark about Leavy being in the hands of the Reynolds brothers, then there is a crack in the organization. We need to know if that's the case, and why that's the case. Let's keep working our own angles. As soon as I work a couple things through, we'll reconvene by phone." Fred disconnects.

"Si, but before we disconnect, I need to address a matter. My apologies Director Webber, but I am going to speak in a way that you won't fully understand. Given the surveillance you are under, I will let John explain in detail at a later time. May I proceed?"

"Of course."

"John, has there been a sighting of novel or spare."

"Not on this end."

"Nor on ours. Thank you, John. Madam Director, I have had lengthy discussions with my cyber team, but I am interested in your thoughts. Using 20/20, we now know that The Realm had two goals: Tango, which appears to be a return on investment program spearheaded by the imprisoned leaders in conjunction with Benton Brettenvue, and the more important goal, the one central to The Body—the possession of the top-ranked cyber huntresses. The taking of Leavy proves The Realm still wants to complete their original goal and weaponize cyberland. The nefarious ones must know they will never get the #1 or #2 huntress off my fortress, so what is the purpose of taking Leavy? While her skills are remarkable, she will be unable to control cyberland because Joy and Annie will negate Leavy's efforts."

Shelby places her hand onto John's, "Rocco, The Realm can run cyberland if they have Leavy doing their hunting and John defending her and blocking Joy and Annie from negating Leavy's efforts. John Maxwell is the next target."

John wraps his fingers with Shelby's.

"Si. That is what John told me when we spoke last night." Rocco ends the call.

Shelby calls out after John as he walks away, "Where are you going?"

"Outside to get your briefcases. Under normal circumstances, you'd be coming down for coffee at this time, so make some noise, do whatever you normally do. When I get back with your things, I'm going to go upstairs and call Agent Rhys. I'll tell her you are being surveilled. You should give her a call in five minutes and keep your conversation brief."

He bounds down the stairs toward the outside.

Shelby calls after him, "John, we need to talk about things."

"Not while the briefcases are in the house," he smirks.

Snowfall Prison

It has been weeks since Leavy was taken. All outward appearances indicate the hostage is accepting her predicament, acclimating to her surroundings, and adhering to the rules Eli sets. Appearances aren't always as they seem.

Every night before she is given her sedative, Eli asks, "What are the rules, Leavy?"

"Don't try to escape. Don't try to engage with others. Don't ask about Manuel." She no longer tears when she recites the rules. Not only does she not ask about Manuel, but she also doesn't allow herself to think about him. Much, anyway. She is steadfast in her belief that he is alive somewhere and looking for her. She counsels herself—lectures herself—"You need to do everything you can to stay alert and alive, so when the time comes to make a move against Eli, or assist others in a rescue, you are ready and able." Firmly in that mindset now, Leavy addresses the cornerstone of survival, "Weaponize whatever you have at your disposal. Being shackled negates most options. The only thing I have to use is me." Day by day, former FICA Agent, Hannah Leavy, takes mental trips back to her training days at Quantico to her weapons training, her hand to hand combat training, her physical fitness and tactical training. She ends each mental session with the recruit's mantra, "An FBI agent does **whatever** it takes to survive."

An analyst by profession, Leavy conducts a compare/contrast assessment of the medical professional who aided her after her concussion with the man who kidnapped her. "Doctor Reynolds was a kind-hearted, attentive man with an Earth-crunchy vibe. Eli Reynolds, the captor, is **not** that dude." She recognizes him now as former military. "He moves with precision, maintains a tight schedule, and controls his surroundings. When he interfaces with me, he is deliberate. He remains outside the reach of my chains, holds his weapon at the ready and confirms he will use it against me. Eli does not want to use his weapon against me. He wants me." She shivers at that awareness. "That gives me an edge over him, slight as it might be."

Reflections.

Rocco heads to the medical suite between telephone meetings with John and Fred. He expects to spend time watching his son on a monitor and is pleasantly surprised when Dr. Weinstock allows him to sit with Manuel.

"He is sedated. You may be with him, but do not touch him or talk to him. No stimulus, please."

Rocco nods. The next few minutes with his boy are the hardest he's spent since Manuel arrived back at The Compound. There are no touches of love and support, no way to soothe the ache that presses deep. The saddened father is alone and untethered and soon lost in thought...

Casella, Italy
1990

"Get up."

Rocco pushed himself off of the ground, charged forward and headbutted a man who took the blow easily. The aggressor landed back on his ass, a gun leveled at his head.

"You need to listen, Fiancetti," the armed man said through clenched teeth, his British accent out of place along the quaint Italian countryside. "Your father contacted your mother and told her about the trouble you and Eleni are in. Despite their animosity toward one another, she accepted his words as truth and dispatched me straight away." The Brit directed Rocco again, "Get up."

He did as he was told, swayed a bit from the effort, but remained upright.

"My name is Mick Bentley. I am MI6. I was hoping to get to you before your wife was abducted, but we only learned of this mess hours ago."

Rocco swayed again.

Mick offered support.

The young man pushed away and began running toward the stone cottage. "My son!"

"Who's inside? I saw you with a man?" Bentley called after him.

"Tomas and his wife Maria. She came to help Eleni with the birth of our boy," his voice cracked.

"Deal with your pain later. Tell me about Tomas and Maria. Do you trust them?" Mick challenged.

"More than I trust you."

"I need to talk to the woman."

Rocco scoffed, "She's a bit unconscious at the moment."

The MI6 operative turned and sprinted toward his car, Rocco stayed tight on his heels and tried to focus on Bentley's directive, "Take your son back to Genoa or to England, Fiancetti. Do not stay here. I'll be in touch."

"You will find her."

"That's the plan."

Rocco blocked the path of the British Intelligence officer. "Bentley, that was not a question. It was a directive. **You. Will. Find. Her.**"

London, England
1990

Mick Bentley addressed Alistair Duff, aka Rocco Fiancetti. "Eleni is back in Santorini, or more precisely she is being held on one of her father's yachts in the South Aegean Sea off the island's coast. Nikos Galanos, Andros Karras' right-hand-man, is her guard and is with her 24/7. We have an operative on the waitstaff who has orders to intervene only if Eleni is threatened in any way. She is completely unaware of this person's duplicity. I have people in the area who report that whenever the yacht moves close to land, Eleni moves to the main deck. We think she is hopeful someone will recognize her and will report back to you. Technically, that is what is happening at this meeting."

"Will there be a rescue attempt?"

"We have no authority in Santorini, certainly none on the yacht of Andros Karras."

"Then why do you have an operative with her?" **Rocco pushed.**

"For her protection. And should a day come when Andros Karras gets in our crosshairs, we will be ready to act."

1995

"There are rumblings about an operation in the South Aegean Sea," SIS Operative Alistair Duff said as he walked uninvited into his boss' office.

Mick said nothing.

"There is only one thing of value in the waters off Santorini—from the standpoint of British national security."

Mick said nothing.

"Andros Karras' fleet of supertankers," Rocco pushed.

Mick said nothing.

"When Eleni was first taken, you said we have no authority in Santorini, certainly none on the yacht of Andros Karras. Has that changed?"

Mick nodded. "SIS will be making a move to get Andros Karras. He has some answering regarding his fleet of supertankers."

Rocco ponders a minute, "Karras is on the yacht with Eleni?"

Mick said nothing.

Rocco took a seat opposite his boss and friend. He leaned forward, put his elbows on his thighs, folded one hand over the other in a near fist and tapped his forefinger across his knuckles. After several minutes he stood, "Mick, this is your dilemma. You put me on the mission or I go rogue. I give you my assurances, I won't interfere with your plans for Andros Karras. I only want Eleni."

Mick opened his desk drawer and pulled a sealed envelope. Alistair Duff's name was written across the front, "Your papers. I put you on the assignment this morning. Report to your field commander."

Rocco is pulled back to the here and now by the touch of his son's hand on his.

Off the grid and in the dark.

Fred gets everyone back onto a conference call. "RFI Cyber Specialist Randy Parker is sending you a video of Mike Monopoli answering my questions about the morning of the shooting and kidnapping. You should review it and make your own assessments. I have already made mine. I'm of the mindset that there was a long game put in place to get the cyber huntresses, but I think Leavy's kidnapping was a seat of the pants decision, and it was initiated by Eli. I agree with John's assessment that the only people who know about Leavy's kidnapping are the Reynolds brothers. I think they are keeping the other Realm members in the dark on this. If that is the case, we are on a very tight timeframe. Eli and Mathis are off the grid. They're most likely not communicating with anyone—including other members of The Realm. There has got to be some worrying going on inside the rank and file. Could be the only thing they know for sure is the son of Rocco Fiancetti is dead, and RFI is highly motivated to find the killer and anyone associated with him. I give it another 24-36 hours before The Realm shit hits the fan. John, I'm on board with you using Leavy to our advantage. Put your plan into play, and keep me apprised. I need to—"

Rocco pushes in before Fred disconnects, "Fred, the RFI cyber division and the three others on this call have been working a question. I'd like your immediate response."

"Shoot."

"The Realm has #3 and they want #2 and #1, but they will never get the other cyber huntresses from my Compound. So, what is their plan?"

"Cyber shit isn't in my wheelhouse, Rocco, but any successful war needs offense and defense. Eli Reynolds has possession of some offense, so you'd better tighten security on your ass, John. Okay, boys and girls, I'm off to work in my own wheelhouse. Be safe out there."

Heading to Philly

Fred places a call from the car, "Granger, it's Fred Serpico."

"I still have caller ID, Detective."

"Still a pisser, sir." They share a laugh. "I'm sorry for the early call, but I'm heading to Philly from Lewisburg. I need to see you and Faye, today, sir."

"Come to our condo. You have the address."

"I should be there in a couple of hours. I'll be bringing Detective Ted Brothers with."

"Very well."

Another call is placed by Fred, "Hey, Brothers."

"I think you mean to say, hey brother." Ted cracks up at his own joke.

"Hey brother. Any chance you can meet me at Granger Mitchell's condo? You can bring Penny if need be."

"What time you looking at, Fred?"

"I'm a couple hours out, so around 10:30."

"Perfect. Penny's physical therapist will be here, so she won't be alone. I'll meet you at Granger's."

Drexel Hill

Layne Osterman has been deep in reconnaissance since she switched out the Camaro. She's been by the detective's house many times, usually making her trips during the morning and evening commutes and at mid-day lunch. One of her targets is turning out to be a static mark. "Penny Meehan hasn't left the residence since I got her in my sights. The injured reporter stays put, and the only visitor she's had is her physical therapist, who arrives for a morning session at 10:30 and finishes up by noon. No reason to think today will be any different."

Layne's other target is a more difficult mark. "Ted Brothers comes and goes infrequently, and when he does leave, his trips are usually five minutes here, five minutes there, except for the times when the therapist is with Penny. The detective leaves the house for that entire block of time." The assassin checks her watch. "Penny has a session in a couple hours. That should put the detective out of the house. That means it's time to pay an unexpected visit, a deadly visit to the physical therapist." Layne parks her borrowed ride as close to the tree line on the tiny cul-de-sac as possible, waits it out, then hoofs it to the sweet little cottage with a blue Honda parked on the driveway.

Twenty-three-year old, Kelly Thompson, never knew what hit her when she exited her back door that morning. She was dead before the screen door slammed behind her. Layne pulls Kelly's body into the shrubs and heads inside. "Twelve minutes to change and get to Brothers' place. Tight, but doable." The assassin enters Kelly's perfectly cared for bedroom, opens a few drawers and takes what she needs. "Medical pants and shirt." She tosses the jacket and wool cap she pulled off the dead chick onto the bed and gets to work. She is changed and in the blue Honda within four minutes. "Right on schedule." She sings her little ditty along the way, "Find a Penny, shoot the fuck, all day long, you'll have good luck."

Lucky.

    Penny is heading toward the stairs at the second-floor landing when she hears Kelly Thompson's car coming down the street. The blue Honda is in desperate need of a muffler and announces itself long before it arrives at the log cabin. The patient grabs a glance out Ted's office window when she reaches the first floor and heads to the front door. She flips open the lock and is suddenly overcome with **that** feeling—the one she got right before Boston tore a hole through her with a high-powered rifle, and the one she got when she woke from a sound sleep to find Mason Trellis breaking into the house—she's currently alone in.

    Penny steals another quick look out Ted's window. "The Honda isn't where Kelly normally parks it." She eyes the woman walking to the front door. "That's not Kelly. Her walk is off. Her energy is off." Penny races to the little area between Ted's office and the den, unlatches the top of a hidden door, and sneaks into the root cellar seconds before the doorbell rings and the front door opens. Penny doesn't move from her perch on the top step.

    The woman calls out, "Hi Penny, it's Kelly."

Silence.

"Hey, Penny, did you forget about our session?"

Silence.

Penny concentrates on the footfalls that move from room to room on the first floor. She pulls and holds a breath when her phone comes to life in the distance. Mary Chapin Carpenter's *I Feel Lucky* fills the kitchen where she'd left her cell. In seconds, the song fades then after a moment of silence the tune begins again. As soon as it stops the house phone rings and a series of clicks puts a big-ass relic of an answering machine to work. Penny strains to hear Ted's voice coming from his office.

"Hey, Lucky. I'm with Fred. Call me back when you finish your therapy. We're bringing pizza."

The footfalls pick up speed, "So you are here, Lucky. Don't plan on having pizza with your guy."

Penny crouches as the assassin runs up to the second floor. She takes that opportunity to move from the top step down into the root cellar. Doors slamming and furniture flipping cover the sounds of her breathing and banging heart. She counts the footfalls as they make their way to the first floor, then holds her breath when movement stops on the other side of the hidden door.

"Where the fuck are you!"

Penny mentally tracks the assassin's movements through the kitchen and out onto the breezeway. She wraps herself tight to ward off the cold, stares at the space heater and imagines it's throwing off heat. A shake takes hold, fueled by the frigid temps, and the sheer terror of the assassin's song.

"Find a Penny, shoot the fuck, all day long, you'll have good luck."

Penny begins whispering, "Ted, please come home. Ted, please come home. Ted. Come. Home."

Philadelphia

Granger Mitchell has a smile on his face when he answers the door.

"Shit," Fred whispers.

"I was going to say hello, Fred, but I'll play along. Shit."

"You look well, Granger."

"One foot in front of the other, Fred."

"Sorry to say, I'm about to knock your feet out from under you."

"Thanks for the warning. Come on in. Now, let's hear why you needed to see Faye and me."

"Should I tread, or would you prefer it straight?" Fred asks.

"Straight, Fred. Always, straight."

Fred nods. "Stacy Remington was the intended target that night."

He lets Granger pull a few breaths, unsteady as they may be.

"There was a death threat levied against her by The Realm, and when she didn't back down from her investigation, they assassinated her."

Granger lets go of Faye's hand and begins looping the living room. On his fifth spin he addresses Fred, "Who?"

"We have a suspect."

"Who?"

"I can't tell you that, Granger."

"Can't or won't?"

"Can't. RFI isn't the only agency working this so I need to stay within a few lanes. The minute I can divulge the name, I will. There's more, will you sit?"

Granger sits with Faye, their hands instinctively find one another.

"Again, this is being given to you straight. The Realm has an elimination list and they've started working through it. First, the two EMTs on scene that night were killed. They were taken out to prevent their confirmation of my testimony that I read Paul Ferraro, aka Boston, his Miranda rights. Second, a Realm associate paid a visit to Ted's house and ended up dead for his troubles. Third, it was Manuel and—"

Ted shoots from the couch, "Penny! Fred. Penny. Follow when you can!"

Fred yells over his shoulder to Mr. and Mrs. Mitchell, "Granger you are on the elimination list. Please go to 275 until I deal with this. Please go."

Drexel Hill

The ring of the house phone and Ted's voice on the answering machine brings hope to her heart. "Penny! Pick up! Pick up! Penny! Where are you? You're in danger! Fred and I are five minutes out. Pick up! Pick up!"

The assassin rages at her hidden victim. "NOOOOO! You fucked up the mission! I'll be back for you and when I take you out, I'm gonna make you suffer."

Penny nearly loses it at the sound of the front door being ripped from its hinges— completely loses it at the sound of Kelly's blue Honda start and speed away. Overcome with fear she searches for a place to hide.

Layne Osterman returns Kelly Thompson's car to her driveway, sprints to the tree line, throws herself in to Sarge's F-150 seconds before a blue and white pulls onto Kelly Thompson's driveway. The murderer waits while the cops knock on the front door then head to the back of the house, before driving from the murder scene.

Ted Brothers' log cabin is destroyed when the men enter. They move from room to room in search of Penny or the intruder. They don't call out to her until they have cleared the house. Ted quickly moves to the tiny area inside the front door and unfastens the latch on the root cellar. It is dark and there is no outward sign that Penny is down there. The men inch down, down, down.

"Lucky, it's Ted and Fred. If you are armed, Lucky, hold your fire. I'm coming to get you." At the bottom step, Ted hears a whimper. He follows the childlike sound to the space under the stairs. He shines a pen light and sees his woman covered in dirt, shaking uncontrollably, racked with convulsing fear. He offers her his hand. "Come on Penny, let me take you upstairs."

She is barely functioning and isn't moving. Ted sits on the floor and begins inching toward her. He gently presses his mass against her and waits for his familiarity to hit home. When it does, she collapses against him.

Fred sprints upstairs, making a path as he moves. He hurriedly straightens the master bedroom, and helps Ted get Penny settled onto the bed. Ted crawls on with her and gently pulls his woman close. She has stopped crying, but is still shaking uncontrollably. She hasn't spoken and her eyes have yet to lose the fear.

"Ted, we need to get her the fuck out of here. Hell, the three of us need to get the fuck out of here. I'm packing your shit and hers. Be ready to move in ten minutes." Fred packs the Jeep with his friends' gear, helps Ted get Penny situated in the back, runs back inside and shuts down Ted's house, pulling shades all around and jacking chairs under every doorknob. Fifteen-minutes after finding Penny they are on the road.

Ted has his Lucky Penny tucked under this arm in the back seat. He whispers and brushes gentle kisses on her head. Long gone are her tears, they've been replaced by a terrifying silence. After many agonizing minutes Fred breaks the silence, "Wanda Johnson is going to meet us at 275. You remember Wanda, right Penny?"

There is no response.

"She helped you get settled after you were discharged from the hospital."

There is no response.

Fred checks the rearview mirror. "Ted, you might want to loosen your grip. She might not be able to register pain and tell you about it. She's still pretty fucked up from the shooting."

Fred's words register somewhere in Penny and she begins a mantra, "Find a penny, find a penny, find a penny…" Those words fill the space until Penny collapses from sheer exhaustion.

275

Mike meets the men at the back entrance, "Ted, take her to apartment 702, Wanda Johnson is waiting."

The physician's assistant tells Ted to put Penny onto the bed. The terrified woman shakes her head violently from side to side and clings onto her man.

"Penny, do you remember me? I helped you get settled at Ted's house when you got out of the hospital."

Penny nods.

"I'd like to examine you and it would be easier if you laid down. Is that something you can do?"

Penny clings tighter to Ted.

Wanda makes gentle contact with her hand onto Penny's arm. "That's alright. How about if Ted lies next to you?"

Penny's hold loosens.

"Good." Wanda begins her exam by feeling for any sign of concussion. She checks the eyes and ears of her patient then runs her fingers along Penny's neck which causes her to wince. "Penny, does your neck hurt when I touch it?"

"Shoulder," Penny responds then begins her mantra again, "Find a penny, find a penny, find a penny."

Snowfall Prison

Things have changed over recent days. The captor and captive move about the space as though each chooses to be there—a ridiculous notion given one of the two people is armed and in control, and the other is shackled and under control. To her credit, Leavy has put on a convincing show of acclimation, adherence, and acceptance; subsequently, she reaps small rewards for her efforts. She is allowed to move throughout the log cabin, so long as she is escorted and chains herself once she reaches her destination. The movement has allowed her to get the lay of the land, both inside and outside her prison. There are two places Leavy finds enjoyable, for lack of a better word, a window seat in a lofted area that provides a view of a wide expanse of snow-covered land, rimmed by deep woods, and the other is an overstuffed plaid couch set near a fieldstone fireplace in a wood-paneled room. It is there that she is allowed to sit and read.

The former agent doesn't know where the log cabin is located, but from her lofted perch she's discerned it is remote and has a snow cover that's easily three feet deep. Nearly every day since her arrival, new snow falls. She welcomes the silent beauty, and when she is feeling particularly brave, she thinks about the walk she and Manuel took during a light snowfall the night before she was taken. This is not one of those times of silent reflection.

"Eli."

"Yes, Leavy."

"It's snowing."

"Yes."

She says nothing more. It has become their way of things. She says it's snowing and he knows she wants to go outside. Her communication style isn't the only thing Eli knows about the woman under his control, and he's made sure he shared his knowledge during her time in captivity...

"We have a selection of music here. Any preference? How about some jazz?" Leavy loves jazz, though she doesn't listen to it often because it reminds her of her parents. "I had the provisions delivery team add ingredients for hot chocolate." Leavy loves hot chocolate. She also loves honey, and wool rag socks, and is partial to the color navy. There is a supply of honey in the cupboard, wool rag socks in her dresser, and her bedroom comforter is navy.

After a few minutes, Eli addresses her comment about the snow. "Would you like to go out in the snow, Leavy?"

"Yes, please."

Hannah Leavy uses her time outside to work her muscles and breathe in fresh, cold air. If she gets the chance to escape, she needs to be in physical shape to do so. On this crisp, clear day as she runs through the snow and tosses snowballs about, she surveys her surroundings and tries really hard to ignore the man standing in the doorway with a loaded gun in his hand.

Let me remove your doubts.

Felicity is on edge. Days have passed with no further communication from Mathis Reynolds, and she hasn't heard anything from Turner Rodgers since the killing of Manuel Xavier. For all she knows, the presidential candidate is dead, too. "That'd be one less fucker to worry about." She needs to do something to lessen her anxiety, so she places a call to Jack McGovern. "I gave you an assignment Jack. Where do we stand?"

"I bugged Webber's office at J. Edgar and her briefcases. They picked up a conversation she had with Maxwell about his hotel being tossed and bugged and his car being GPS trapped. We have his J. Edgar office bugged, so when he's there he's under surveillance, but he's been giving us the slip after hours. He's not driving his car, and as far as we can tell he's doing single night stays at hotels."

"Are you sure he's not staying with Webber?"

"Nothing to suggest it, but the bugs had the desired effect. Maxwell hasn't been to the Bureau for days. And Webber hasn't been in since I tapped her briefcases. She probably thinks her house is the only place without ears. She's wrong, so it's just a matter of time before she says something useful."

"Keep me in the loop, Jack. I've got a call coming in. Felicity Ferraro."

"This is Mathis Reynolds. I have some things that need to be taken care of ……. are you still there, Mrs. Ferraro?"

"Yes."

"I detect hesitancy. Perhaps you are not convinced of my role in The Realm. Let me remove your doubts. I know the location of your young children."

Felicity's gasp is loud and immediately silenced by a knot in her throat.

"Have I passed your test, Mrs. Ferraro?"

"Yes."

"Very well. Turner Rodgers will not be communicating with you or the Gang of Eight for the foreseeable future. There is an upcoming presidential election and it is imperative that he be seated in the Oval Office. You may continue to use him as your supposed handler for purposes of explanation to the others, however all future orders will come from me and be delivered by you. Do you understand, Mrs. Ferraro?"

"Yes."

"Very well. The next matter concerns your husband. He has been informed of your more expanded role within the organization and the cessation of prison visits from you—legal and conjugal."

There is another noticeable intake of air by Felicity.

"You are a beautiful woman. I am sure your bed won't be empty for very long. Are you still with me, Mrs. Ferraro?"

"Yes."

"Very well. Two more things. Tell Jack McGovern that John Maxwell needs 24/7 surveillance. I want it in place within 24 hours. And from now on, speak only to people with whom I instruct. Is that understood, Mrs. Ferraro?"

"Yes."

"I have eyes and ears on you. That is all, Mrs. Ferraro."

She is still holding the phone in her trembling hand when she receives a text. It contains a video of her four-year-old twins sitting on a rock at the water's edge, surrounded by a lush forest. The tykes are dressed for a day of woodland exploring with little binoculars hanging from their necks, and wide-brimmed hats covering their heads. Rainboots with cartoon frogs and turtles show signs of recent water play. The boy and girl are holding their tiny hands in the air and waving to the camera. Their little singsong voices calling out, "Hi, Mommy. We love you."

Felicity dies inside.

DC Correctional Treatment Facility
Paul Ferraro receives a message delivered by a Realm runner inside the jail. The message is that his wife's visit has been postponed. Paul wants to rage, but he knows better. He stuffs his shit down and asks the Correctional Officer if he knows when she will be in to see him.

"Not sure. The message about today's cancellation just came in. I'll let you know when a new visitation request is filed."

Paul knows he'll never see Felicity or his children again. He readies himself for death.

Woman, this cussing thing.

       Fred is in Malcolm and Gretchen's penthouse staring out a bank of windows overlooking Hufnagle Park and Market Street. He's expecting Granger and Faye Mitchell, and he's processing some anxiety over their delayed arrival. After the assassin visited Ted Brothers' place in search of Penny, he had second thoughts about the Mitchells traveling alone, so he sent Mike Monopoli and Randy Parker to their place the night before. Fred relaxes when the transport vehicle turns onto Market Street, relaxes more when the privacy elevator pings and the door opens.

       He hangs back while the relatives do the whole 'good to see you' thing. When Gretchen finally gets around to asking about the unexpected visit, Granger and Faye turn their eyes toward Fred. Gretchen follows their line of vision

       "Oh for fuck's sake, now what?" she groans.

       "Gretchen," her father admonishes.

       "Sorry, Daddy, but whenever you and that one over there are in the same room there's some trouble brewing. If you don't appreciate my foul mouth, I suggest you keep him from putting me in a foul mood."

Fred laughs from across the room. "See, Granger, she's a pisser just like you."

Malcolm, who has been holding up the brick wall, pushes off, "Fred, I suggest you tell my woman what she wants to know."

"You all talk amongst yourselves for a few. Randy and Mike will busy themselves with rearranging furniture. There's a 275 meeting in ten minutes."

"There better be dancing, Fred."

"If you don't interrupt me, Gretchen, I'll take you for a spin after the meeting," he laughs. "No way that'll be happening," he whispers.

Gretchen is perched on the comfy leather couch when Fred brings in the team. Everyone takes seats and Fred takes center stage. "This is catch up time. Some of you already know some of what's going on, but this meeting will let all of you know where we stand. Most of what I say will be new. What is not new, boys and girls, is that I do not like to be interrupted."

"We know!" is chorused back.

Fred chuckles, "Good. First, an update on Penny Meehan. She is currently resting under the watchful eye of Damian and Wanda Johnson. She is mostly uncommunicative. As best we can tell, a contracted assassin posing as her physical therapist gained entry to Ted Brothers' home while he was away. Something must have alerted Penny to danger because she escaped to a hidden root cellar, which is where Ted and I found her after her ordeal. From the looks of things, the assassin hunted that poor woman and destroyed Ted's home in the process.

"We did not report the event to the authorities. The police never would have allowed us to take Penny and there was no way we were staying or leaving her behind. She is under our protection until further notice. Ted and Penny will be staying in apartment 702. As soon as Wanda says she can have visitors, I'd like that to happen. Don't expect much by way of chit-chat, but let's spend some time with her. And Gretchen, if you could ease her in before you go all word mashup that would be great."

"I can practice now with only two words for you, Fred."

He laughs big. "You're a pisser, Gretchen."

She gives him one of her smiles.

He continues.

"Okay, boys and girls, it's quiet time. Malcolm keep a watch on your wife; she is going to become agitated. Faye, do the same with your husband. I have four main topics. The first pertains to the shooting of Stacy Remington. After an RFI 20/20 review, we have concluded that she was the intended target that night at the Cottage on Old Estate Road. In the days preceding the shooting, The Realm issued a death threat against Stacy which prompted the Director of the FBI to bench her from The Realm investigation. This move resulted in RFI's benching. Stacy continued her work which pissed off The Realm. They used intelligence they gathered from their surveillance of the director to hijack the trap we set for the assassin known as Boston. They turned our 'lure and capture' plan into an opportunity to assassinate Stacy Remington."

All eyes turn to Gretchen, "I'm alright, please keep going, Fred."

"RFI can pull this case apart seven ways to Sunday and find places where we fell short and where we need to make improvements. And we will do that, but it won't change the bottom line. The Realm had everything they needed to fuck up our plan because they had access to Stacy's home files and all of our conversations. They had that access because they had Stacy under surveillance—in her townhouse—for years."

Fred turns to Granger, "When you and I met yesterday, you wanted me to tell you who ordered the killing of Stacy. I couldn't tell you at that time, but I've had a conversation with an important player in this shit show and I have been given authority to disclose what we have uncovered."

Granger gasps when the realization hits. Doubles over from the shock of it. Fred moves to the man, "You need to calm down, Granger. Your suspicions are correct, but you need to calm down."

Granger can't calm down. He is nearing a full-blown attack of some sort.

"Randy, get Wanda. Now. Tell her to bring her medical bag."

Faye steps back as Fred gets into Granger's face. "We are going to get him. You need to calm down so you can be with us when we do. Granger, pull it together." Fred has his hand on Granger's wrist, when Wanda enters the room he says, "Pulse over 140."

"Everyone except Faye out," Wanda orders. "That includes you Gretchen." As the team begins to leave, Wanda spews, "I should set up a damned clinic at 275. I could make a financial killing."

The team isn't even at the entertainment room when Gretchen begins, "What the fuck is going on, Fred?"

Malcolm speaks up, "Woman, this cussing thing. Do you plan on continuing it when DelRae gets here?" He sits next to her.

"Oh, good Lord, my husband is sitting. What the eff .... what the hell is going on, Malcolm?"

He takes her hands in his. "Fred knows who the head of The Realm is, and Granger just figured it out. The person who is responsible for all of this mess, the killing of Stacy, the shooting of Manuel, the kidnapping of Leavy, and everything else is Mathis Reynolds."

Gretchen's head practically 360s from her neck. She finds Fred, who nods. Her thoughts zoom to her father and she begins to cry. "Oh, Malcolm, Daddy's heart can't take the shock or pain of this. I need to be with him, please."

"Fred, check with Wanda," Malcolm directs.

Several minutes later the detective returns, "We can head to the living room."

When they enter, Granger stands and addresses the team, "Faye and I will be adjourning to the guest suite at the advice of Wanda Johnson." Granger walks to his daughter, "I am taking care of myself by leaving this room. If you need to follow suit to take care of you and DelRae, please do so." Granger places a kiss on Gretchen's head, "I love you."

Gretchen watches her Daddy walk away. His arm casually slung over his wife's shoulder.

Malcolm disrupts his wife's gaze, "I think you should leave. I'll follow you in a few minutes and tell you what's going on. Please, Woman."

Gretchen places her hand onto her baby ball and turns to Wanda. "You're going to check me and DelRae out, aren't you?"

"Yes. And I'm trusting that Fred will keep my patient load to three this evening: Granger, Gretchen, and DelRae."

"Yes, ma'am," Fred calls after the diminutive darling.

Fred picks up the pace, "I'm gonna do an information dump. We're all staying at 275, so we can ask and answer questions later. The most important thing for you all to know is that Mathis Reynolds is The Body. We think the brothers are off the grid and at least one of them is with Leavy. Eli playacted a thing for Leavy when he was treating her for her concussion, so she's probably with him. For her sake, I hope his interest in her was an act.

"The next topic is gonna send Gretchen off, Malcolm, so tread lightly. Everyone at the

Cottage the night of Stacy's assassination is on an elimination list. The Realm is taking out people one by one. So far, we have two dead EMTs, and an RFI detective who barely survived a shooting, but who the world thinks is dead. Penny would have died by an assassin's bullet if not for luck, ingenuity, and grit, and I suspect the assassin would have killed Ted upon his arrival home. Since Granger was at the shooting scene, he and Faye can't be left alone. They will be staying here for a few days, and a plan will be put in place for their 24/7 protection. That leaves the following people on the elimination list. Fred Serpico, Mike Monopoli, and Steve Phelps. And unless I'm completely off the mark, The Realm assassin, Paul Ferraro, is at the top of the hit list."

Word mashes and wet murmurs.

The Mayor makes an early morning announcement to the hodgepodge squatters at 275, "For the foreseeable future, RFI business will be conducted in the Diving Center or in the apartments on the seventh floor. The penthouse living space is designated Christmas Central."

Gretchen doesn't miss a beat. "Before any of you well-built men thunder from the living quarters know this. I will have your assistance with the stringing of pretty things, so come willingly or deal with 77. You are dismissed."

The men dash away, dash away, dash away, all.

Faye laughs at the display, then turns her attention to other important things. "I walked through DelRae's nursery and playroom this morning. The construction team did a wonderful job laying the carpet, and the painted moldings look beautiful against the painted brick. It's really a lovely place, Gretchen."

"It is beautiful. I can't wait to put the furniture together. Boxes and boxes have been arriving so with some work the place should be set before baby ball arrives," she enthusiastically rubs her belly.

"I bet you're excited about seeing the finished product," Faye gives a little giggle.

Gretchen beams, "I can't wait to see her crib and changing table and rocker and such, but I'm over the moon about her layette." Gretchen pulls a long happy breath, "Oh, Faye, you're right, I can't wait to see the finished product, as you say."

Faye takes Gretchen's hand, "I was referring to DelRae," she smiles wide.

"Oh, Faye, I can hardly contain myself. The last few weeks of pregnancy are nearly unbearable. I've taken to fantasizing about DelRae when I'm awake and when I'm asleep. Did I ever tell you about a dream I had about the baby?"

"I don't think so."

"In my dream DelRae is about nine months old, and she is sitting on Malcolm's knee. She is all arms and legs moving about, and smiling this wide, near-toothless grin at her daddy. She's lighter-skinned than Malcolm, but favors him very much. She has a head full of black springy curls and the biggest round cornflower blue eyes. I'm telling you Faye; DelRae is the most beautiful thing in all the world. I just know that's what she looks like. I just know it."

"Pardon my interruption," Granger says as he joins the women, "Gretchen, your mother had a similar dream about you shortly before your birth. Delaney went into a full description of what you would look like on your first birthday. She and I remarked on the day of your Winnie the Pooh celebration how spot on she was." The father places a connecting touch upon his daughter's shoulder.

"Winnie the Pooh," the mother-to-be whispers.

Granger's smile warms Gretchen's heart as she quietly recites the first few lines from her most favorite Pooh quote. It's one that holds her most cherished childhood memories. "You are braver than you believe ~ stronger than you seem." She pulls a shaky breath.

"Gretchen, come here."

The beaming daughter pushes herself from her seat and goes to her daddy. "I'm so happy we are all together." The contentedly embraced daughter spies Fred walking toward them, "I'm happy, even if he's around."

"You're a pisser, Gretchen. Just wanted to let you know that I'm receiving a delivery and it needs to come up the elevator. Should be here any minute."

Gretchen takes Faye's hand, "Let's get out of the way." The women head to the comfy couch by the window and are barely seated when the ping of the elevator draws their attention. Mike and Ted step off lugging the most gorgeous 9' Canadian Blue Spruce tree.

Gretchen squeals her delight.

Fred explains. "The RFI team chose this tree from The Compound, cut it, and sent it. We want you to know how much we appreciate your friendship. This is the first of what will be an annual tradition, Mrs. Mayor."

Gretchen is so focused on Fred that she's missed the joining of everyone at 275 for this momentous occasion. Even Penny has ventured out of 702 for the first time since arriving. Gretchen gets up and walks to the beautiful black haired woman with dark chocolate eyes that bear the signs of too many tears.

"We've never met. I'm Gretchen Mitchell, and I'm so pleased you are well enough to join us, Penny." The woman of the manor addresses Randy, "Would you mind spinning the comfy couch so Penny and I can watch the men set the tree?"

Not only did the men set the tree, but they strung it with lights and helped Faye with the ornaments. As the men placed an ornament here, Faye moved it there. Here. There. Here. There. Many minutes passed before the detectives detected what was happening, which brought the women of the manor to fits of laughter, which turned into a bout of tears for Penny.

"I'm sorry, Gretchen."

"You're entitled to your tears and your fears, Penny. I went through a similar experience with a hitman, right downstairs in the garage, nearly lost my life in a not-so-accidental hit and run. And then right over there, at that elevator, a knife-wielding dreg of humanity tried to punish Malcolm by killing me. Now I suppose if you measure the totality of things and the manner and means of intended homicides we'd find differences, but the events were similar in the fright they caused, and I'd like to help, if I can—" Gretchen's word mash is abruptly halted by Randy.

"Geez, Mrs. Mayor, maybe you could shush or something."

Gretchen takes hold of the teary woman's hand, "I tend to ramble."

Penny smiles, then finds Ted's eyes across the room. He sends a smile and holds her stare until she turns to Gretchen, "I do need someone to talk to if you are willing, and if it won't cause you and your baby stress."

"DelRae," Gretchen places her hand to her baby ball, "that's our daughter's name."

"That's lovely." A dawning hits Penny. "It's a mashup of your mother's name, Delaney Rae."

Penny drops her head, shame finding its place on her face. "I'm sorry I caused you and Malcolm so much pain with my research."

"That's water, Penny."

"Water?"

"You know, under the bridge or over the damn or wherever water goes. We are well beyond any of that. You should be, too."

Penny finds Ted's face. He hasn't taken his eyes off the woman who has found, mended, and captured his heart. He winks at his Lucky Penny. She excuses herself and walks towards him, stretches to place a kiss on his cheek and whispers, "I need you, Ted. I need to be brought fully back to you, please."

The man takes hold of his woman's hand and lets her lead the way.

702

Penny's mind and body are fighting for control as her man begins to reclaim her. His caresses, kisses, and murmurs of sweet nothings relax her, but memories slip in and grab hold. She tenses and becomes still as death when the assassin's ditty begins its hateful loop. He starts to pull away. She pulls him near, welcomes him with touches and kisses, "Please, Ted." He positions himself over her, and she nears a full-on panic. He quickly moves off the bed.

"Lucky, this needs to wait. I don't want you to be afraid of me, and I don't want you to hurt yourself, physically or emotionally." When her tears begin and ramp up he goes to her, helps her from the bed. They stand for several quiet minutes, just holding one another until the panic subsides.

Penny takes Ted's hand and leads him to the shower. "I need this, Ted, but I need to take control." She pushes away memories of assassins and root cellars, and welcomes memories of their first time together.

"Sweater off."

He complies.

"Now the jeans."

He groans low when she steps forward and takes him in her hand.

"Undress me, Ted."

She presses her naked self against his length, "I need this." She moves away, turns on the shower and steps in. She puts her back to the spray, offers her hand, and when he joins her, she leans him gently against the wall. She lathers him, slicks the length of him, and cups water in her hands to rinse him. Her kisses and touches bring him to a painful need. She shuts off the water, "Kneel." She positions herself in front of him, puts her feet on either side of his legs and lowers herself. She eases down and guides him in. The woman in control rocks and nestles, raises and lowers, owns his length and when her sexual joy hits, it is immediately followed by his sexual reclamation.

Doppelgangers and listening devices.

FICA Director John Maxwell is in his GPS trapped Escalade, headed to a meeting with FBI Director Shelby Webber. He pulls to the gate, announces his arrival, and drives through the opening security barrier. He laughs at the process. "Dog and pony show."

Once inside, Shelby directs him to the kitchen area, "I was working at the farmer's table. Why don't we go there?"

He takes a seat on one side with she on the other. A briefcase sits between them, the hanging zipper listening device doing what it is intended to do—hanging and listening.

"Director Webber, I've spoken with Rocco Fiancetti and he is out for blood. He knows, we know, hell, everyone in the world knows it was The Realm who took out Manuel."

"Yes. I saw Mr. Fiancetti's reaction the day he came here to sign the release papers for his son's body. He made no attempt to hide his anger or his plan for revenge. What is the purpose of this discussion, Director?"

"He asked that I deliver a request."

"Proceed."

"He wants his team back inside Stacy Remington's townhouse."

Webber ponders. "The townhouse has been put under my jurisdiction, so I am able to grant his request. Did he say what he hopes to find?"

"They'll be searching for evidence regarding the shooting of Director Remington, and the missing pieces we discussed the other day."

John points upwards.

Shelby nods, "Before I make my decision, there's something I'd like your opinion on. The case files are in my home office." They leave the bugged kitchen and when she closes the door she demands an explanation, "What's going on? I thought you were going to drop information about Leavy."

"I have a tail, actually I have several tails. I'm concerned if I drop the dime on Leavy tonight my shadows might make a move on me. If the Reynolds brothers are the only ones who know about Leavy's kidnapping and Jack McGovern finds out he and the other members have been kept in the dark he's going to be pissed, maybe pissed enough to take me and force me to tell him what happened to Leavy. Once he has me, he'll use me as a bargaining chip … you know, because I'm the world's best cyber defender," he smirks.

She ignores his playful attempt. "You work for the FBI John. I'm sure I can get you protection."

"No disrespect ma'am, but the FBI had guards on the Carriage House on Old Estate Road when Celia Brettenvue was murdered. The FBI didn't know one of their senior level directors was working behind the scenes on a case from which she'd been removed. And the deputy director of the FBI is spying on the whole dammed Bureau and is planning the abduction of a senior level director of the FBI. I'm inclined to go outside for protection. I've got some personal stake in this game, namely my ass, and I want people around me who I trust completely."

Shelby concedes with a terse nod, "What's your plan?"

"I'll wrap up tonight's meeting without mentioning Leavy's kidnapping. I'll also say that Rocco has something big he's working on and will bring us into the loop tomorrow. You suggest we reunite at the same time and place tomorrow evening. After I leave, contact Rocco and tell him we are delaying the information drop on Leavy until tomorrow night. I'll follow up with him about the circumstances of that decision and ask for some backup. When I leave here I'm going to drive to a hotel, be seen registering for a room, and seen entering an elevator. I will not be seen getting the fuck out of that hotel and back here, if you will allow that, ma'am."

"I don't like this, Director Maxwell."

"Aw, it's kinda fun. Two would-be lovers kept apart by villainous forces. *He* finds a way onto her estate. *She* peers down at him from her glass wrapped residential prison…"

"That's enough. Let's get back to my briefcase."

"I've been meaning to ask, is it Prada?"

"I do not look like Meryl Streep."

"Actually, you're her doppelganger, circa Out of Africa." He growls low, "That hair washing scene." He growls low again. He thinks he might have seen a lift of Shelby's lip and a dimple of her cheek as she exited the home office. He growls once again.

John starts the ruse when they are within briefcase listening range. "Director, you'll send me portions of those files so I can review them at length?"

"They'll be forwarded by Agent Rhys tomorrow. In the meantime, I'll call Mr. Fiancetti to let him know I will grant his request for entry to Remington's residence the day after tomorrow."

"Christmas?"

"Yes, they don't have to go to Stacy's on Christmas, but they'll have access. They should coordinate with you, Director Maxwell, unless you have plans."

"I'll handle it Director."

"Good. I still want to discuss the other Realm matter with him while you are present, so why don't you and I meet here tomorrow evening."

"Is that all, Director Webber?"

"Yes. See yourself out." Shelby places a call to Rocco as she moves upstairs out of range of the listening device.

The Compound

Rocco takes the call despite his desire to spend a few minutes with Manuel. "Director."

"It's late, I know, but there's a bump in our road. Director Maxwell came to my home this evening to give our listeners information on the Leavy kidnapping. Unfortunately, he brought along several tails with him. He was quite sure if he mentioned Leavy tonight he'd be gone as soon as he ventured back outside."

"He is right. Director. I have not yet informed Fred Serpico of tonight's plan, so the delay is acceptable. Goodnight, Madam Director."

Don't.

Doctor Weinstock nods to Rocco when he enters what is now referred to as the medical suite. "You may sit with Manuel. He is asleep. No touching, no talking."

That leaves Rocco with only one thing to do...

Santorini, Greece
1995

Mick Bentley and his team watched through high powered lenses as the imbedded operative delivered dinner to the ship's bridge, set the tray on a table, pulled a gun, and ordered the captain away from the controls. The officer reached for a weapon. The operative shot him dead, locked down the bridge, and steered the yacht toward land.

The SIS team turned their focus to Nikos Galanos and Eleni who were making their way to Andros Karras' stateroom. "Quiet," Mick ordered, "our operative should be activating sound in a..."

Eleni stopped at the door, her arms folded across her chest, "I'm not hungry."

"Then don't eat. You will sit, Eleni. There are things to discuss."

Eleni remained standing at the door. "The days for discussion are long behind us. You have something to say, so say it."

Before a single word was spoken, the father and daughter felt a push of forward momentum. Dinnerware and glasses slid from the table and crashed across the floor. The engines pushed harder; Andros was thrown back against the chair from which he stood.

"Let's move!" Mick yelled to his SIS team.

Eleni grabbed hold of the door handle just as Nikos pushed into the room. "Mr. Karras, control of the yacht has been seized."

"Get it back!"

"The hijacker is in a bulletproof enclosure. Motorized boats are approaching, the yacht will be boarded. Follow me."

Andros grabbed hold of Eleni who struggled to free herself. He dragged her through the door and toward the deck. "Have you notified our emergency team?" Andros yelled to Nikos.

"The helicopter is two minutes out!" **Nikos yelled back.**

Eleni pulled hard against the hand that bound her wrist, "I won't go."

Andros stopped long enough to backhand her across the face, "You are coming with me. You will never again have the chance to whore yourself out. You will stay with me and never again see your bastard son."

Nikos and Eleni shared a look, he shook his head no, she turned stunned eyes to her father.

"Yes, I know!" **Andros bellowed.** "You have betrayed me, both of you."

"And **you** have stolen a wife from her husband and a mother from her son. A son who has great honor!"

"Husband? You married?"

Eleni dropped to the floor taking pleasure that her words stunned her father. He grabbed hold of her hair and began dragging her, stopping only when she became immovable. He addressed Nikos, who was urging them on, "Give me your gun, Nikos," **he demanded.**

Nikos shook his head, "Get on the helicopter, Mr. Karros. I will bring Eleni to you."

"Give me your gun!" **Andros grabbed the gun from the denying man and immediately fired** a round into his head then trained the weapon on his daughter, **"Get. Up."**

Eleni pushed herself from the floor.

"Get in front of me Eleni. Move toward the helipad," the deranged Andros demanded.

Armed men ascended the lower part of the yacht. From somewhere deep inside Eleni knew Rocco was one of the men boarding the ship. She spun free of her father and ran to the deck's railing, climbed quickly and readied herself for her dive to freedom.

Her father screamed from behind, "I will shoot you dead, Eleni!"

She turned to her father, "You killed me years ago!" She turned back toward the waters and began her dive—just as her father's bullet tore through her.

Rocco raced across the deck and over the side. He pulled a dying Eleni into his arms, desperate to keep her afloat.

"Love," she coughed. "You," she struggled. "Baby," she whispered on her dying breath.

"Eleni! No!" he cried out.

Rocco is pulled from his thoughts when Manuel's medical equipment begins beeping and he begins thrashing.

"Leavy! No!" Manuel calls out.

The doctor moves to his patient's IV to sedate him.

Manuel grabs hold of Weinstock's hand, "Don't."

The doctor lowers his hand when Rocco touches his son's shoulder and repeats his son's directive, "Don't."

Snowfall Prison

Leavy has showered and is ready for bed. She's chained herself, is seated, and has her back to the doorway as is expected of her. She's had a long day and is ready for the sedative she's been given every night since her arrival. She suspects she is addicted to the tiny pills that strip away her awareness of the place she calls, Snowfall Prison. She doesn't care about that. What she cares about is the back and forth flyover of a helicopter earlier in the day, the rise of chimney smoke in the thick of trees outside her loft window, and the snowmobiles that drove past the cabin before bedtime. "I'm not sure how deep into the woods that chimney is, but I'm sure it's east of here, and the entrance to the tree line is a thousand yards or more from the cabin." Leavy stops wondering about helicopters, chimneys, and tree lines when she hears Eli and another man talking. She leans back, straining to hear.

"Consider this an early Christmas present," the visitor says.

Leavy panics inside.

Eli enters her room, stepping well within her circle of chain length. She remains seated.

"Good. I am pleased that you are not looking for an opening to escape. We have company, which is why I have come to you tonight."

The dread of understanding runs Leavy's spine.

Eli smiles, "You understand what this evening is about. This can happen one of two ways, Leavy. Make no mistake, it is going to happen. The man outside is armed and will enter this room at the slightest indication of trouble. Do you understand?"

Leavy hangs her head low—remembers her training—*An FBI agent does **whatever** it takes to survive.*

"With consent there is no need for pain." He bends and unlocks her chains. He pulls her to her feet, palms her cheeks, runs his thumb across the contours of her face, then wraps his hand around the back of her head and meets her for a kiss. It is a memorable first kiss, if one wished to remember it. Leavy does not. She remembers what matters. ***Whatever*** *it takes to survive.*

Eli's desire for Leavy presses hard against her abdomen. She feels it, fears it. *Do **whatever** it takes to survive.* He pulls her top over her head, takes her breasts in his hands, molds them, lifts them, begins kissing, licking, teasing. Her nipples betray her.

"Sit on the edge of the bed."

She obeys.

He runs his hands along her thighs to her waist, slips his fingers into the waistband and pulls off her bottoms. "Spread your legs. Wider. I want to taste you Leavy and then I want you wrapped around me."

A single tear falls as Eli kisses, licks, and sucks the place that Manuel claimed as his own, the place she gave willingly to him. She imagines Manuel's face, his touch. She hears Eli's voice, feels his touch. She knows what is expected of her. She struggles with the line between memory and reality, with the knowledge of what is being done to her and by whom. She denies her body's response. It obeys her, then it betrays. *Do whatever.*

Eli senses her readiness. He pulls his tongue away, strips away his pants, covers her with his body, and enters her. *Whatever it takes.* He takes her persistently and deeply—holds himself until he feels her tighten around him. *To survive.*

He loses himself in her.

Leavy dies inside.

Swings and things.

"Felicity Ferraro," answers the early morning call.

"I trust you delivered my directive to Jack McGovern and you have information to share."

"Yes."

"Proceed."

"John Maxwell had a meeting at Shelby Webber's home in Alexandria. He told her Rocco Fiancetti is seeking retribution for the murder of his son, and that he requested permission for the RFI team to reenter Stacy Remington's residence."

"Was there a stated purpose?"

"Jack characterized it at a fishing expedition on the shooting, but they were looking for something regarding another matter, as well. Something about missing pieces. There were no further details on that."

"Webber's response?"

"She told Maxwell she'd call Fiancetti and grant his request. The RFI team will have access to Remington's townhouse sometime tomorrow."

"Anything further?"

"No."

"Very well, Mrs. Ferraro. Keep the pressure on Jack McGovern. Remind him that you are both being surveilled."

Immediately after disconnecting Felicity receives a video text. This time her twins are on swings affixed to a thick tree branch, their tiny bottoms barely causing a bend in the black rubber seats, their kicking legs pumping off-rhythm. They squeal in delight as they singsong, "Push, please, high, high."

Felicity dies inside.

Burning down the house.

John Maxwell storms the hall, "Shelby get up! Shelby!"

"What the hell, John!" she says from inside, and then again when she opens the door.

"The Remington and Reynolds townhouses are burning to the ground. Get dressed."

The directors arrive on scene to an already fully engulfed building. John leans back against Webber's SUV, the intense inferno cutting the frigid air. Shelby paces back and forth glancing intermittently at the crumbling brick façade and scowling at her companion.

John is about to say something, stops when Jack McGovern appears out of nowhere. Webber wants to rip into the deputy director, takes a step toward him. John pushes off the vehicle and deflects Webber's rage. "Fucking mess, Jack."

"We should have gotten Stacy's stuff out of there when we had the chance, John."

"We did," Maxwell casually lies.

"We did? When?"

John takes his lie for a ride. "I was recently reminded there is a treasure trove of who knows what in Stacy's home office. After a discussion with Director Webber, I ordered the removal of Remington's files and computers. My agents finished up a few hours ago. Anyone who needs to review Director Remington's belongings needs to go through me."

"And RFI?"

John and Shelby let Jack's slip pass. John covers by asking, "Is Mr. Reynolds on scene?"

"I haven't seen him, but I just arrived."

Shelby gets in on the lie-game, "Mathis Reynolds is staying at an undisclosed location. I informed him about the fire, but suggested it was best not to come. I'll let him know both residences are a total loss."

The three watch in silence for several minutes.

"Director Webber, do you require my services?"

Shelby shakes her head, "No, Jack. There's nothing to do. Let's all roll."

John shuts Shelby's car door and heads around to the passenger side. He slams the door shut, "Nice lie about Mathis Reynolds."

She begins to say something, he raises his hand.

"I need a minute." He takes five. "Okay, I don't think Jack McGovern has any idea that Mathis Reynolds is The Body."

"He doesn't," Shelby adds with certainty.

"How do you know?"

"I know Jack's tell—a slight pursing of his lips, followed by a sniff."

"Kind of a big tell," John smirks. "No one's called him on it?"

"I've found it rather advantageous, so I've let it slide," she smiles wide. "Now, what's your second point of discussion?"

"I can't go back to your place. Jack is on the streets and since I'm riding with you, he only has to follow one car. Take me to J. Edgar, my Escalade is there, I'll figure something out for tonight." They ride in silence and are almost at the Bureau when he gets a hinky feeling. "You can't go home, Shelby, at least not alone."

The directors leave her SUV in the garage at FBI Headquarters, grab a cab, exit it a mile from her house and hoof it to her property line. John takes hold of her hand and leads her into a thick of trees and to the breach onto her property.

"A tree? The big reveal of John Maxwell's super spy skills is an overhanging branch?" Shelby scoffs.

"Use what you've got. It's written in the FBI manual, ma'am," John smirks, takes hold of her waist and hoists her high.

Christmas Eve

Chevy Chase

Felicity Ferraro is woken by a pre-dawn call from Jack McGovern. "What?"

"The townhouses owned by Stacy Remington and Mathis Reynolds burned to the ground this morning. When I showed up on scene, Webber and Maxwell were already there. I threw out an off-the-cuff comment that it was too bad the Bureau didn't get Stacy's things before the inferno. Maxwell said he had already ordered the removal of her files and computers and the retrieval had already taken place."

"I thought RFI wanted into the townhouse to do some digging."

"RFI wasn't mentioned, but Maxwell said anyone who wants to review Stacy's stuff has to go through him. Fiancetti and his team can have at it starting tomorrow, but it's a crapshoot if they'll start their work on Christmas. The good news is this, as soon as the RFI investigators starting working with Remington's stuff we'll know where the stash is being kept."

Felicity knows, before she even looks, that the incoming call is from The Body. She disconnects from McGovern. "Felicity Ferraro."

"My home is in ruins."

"Yes."

"Does that mean the RFI problem has been taken care of?"

"No."

"There had better be a good explanation, Mrs. Ferraro."

Lewisburg

A beautifully decorated tree on Christmas Eve morn has ushered in the holiday spirit and lightened Gretchen's home and heart. Her due date is just on the horizon and she is energized, happily nesting, and full of holiday cheer. A Christmas tune is tripping from her lips as she sprinkles red and green sugars onto snowflake and candy cane shaped cookies.

Malcolm comes up from behind his woman and wraps his arms tight. "I have a surprise."

"I believe I feel your surprise against my bottom," she giggles.

"Woman. I need you bad, but that is not a surprise. Come with me."

The mother-to-be and her baby ball lean back against the arm of the couch, her legs stretch the length of it. Malcolm takes them onto his lap and runs his hands up her shins. "Damn, Woman, there's some prickly stuff here."

"Can't bend. Can't shave. It's your fault, so deal."

Malcolm smiles and places his hand on their baby, "She sure was a surprise."

"An unplanned blessing."

"Yes. Two blessings this year. I'm a lucky man, Gretchen."

"I was just saying that to Faye. Not that you were blessed, though you are, but that I was doubly blessed. So much has happened this year, some good, some not so good, and some downright terrifying, but we needn't drudge all that up again, although I did a bit of drudging with Penny. I was trying to make her feel better by telling my experiences with the dastardlies as Randy calls them, but you know me, I sort of got into it, but as fortune would have it Randy was there to put a..."

"Good lord, Woman, quiet down. I want to tell you a bit about a surprise I have for the three girls in my life."

Gretchen smiles. "How curious. I was unaware that my husband has two other girls in his life. I have to say, Mr. Mayor, I'm not at all pleased with this surprise so far."

"Woman, be still. Mama Girl is alone too often. I haven't been with her in any measurable way since the election, and with DelRae's birth just around the corner, I'll have even less time with Mama Girl. I hope you might consider having…"

"Mama Girl move into the guest suite. Oh, Malcolm, that is a wonderful idea. Let's kick Mr. and Mrs. Mitchell to the curb so we can start decorating. We only have today to pull this gift together. And with Mama Girl coming for Christmas, we'll be able to surprise her real good, and…"

"Gretchen. Slow your roll and listen. When I lived in Texas, I had a room at the ranch for Mama Girl. She stayed there a few times and said it was filled with wonderous things. I contacted Sammi Wilcox at Wyldwood and asked that she pull the bedroom pieces out of storage and send them. I explained my plan to Granger and Faye and they readily and happily moved to an apartment on the seventh floor. Faye pulled me aside and said she needed something to do with her time and asked if she could help. I turned the decorating project over to her."

"Malcolm, you are a wonderful man."

"You won't think so in a minute. You are banned from the guest suite. I want it to be a surprise for you and Mama Girl."

"But."

"No buts, Gretchen. Mama Girl is coming tomorrow morning. You can wait until Christmas before you go butting in. Besides, Faye has some work still to do."

"Fine."

"Mrs. Mayor, until further notice you are not allowed beyond our bedroom walls. Is that understood."

"Bully."

"Understood?"

"Dictator."

"Understood?"

"Tyrant."

"Understood, Woman?"

"Understood."

Malcolm moves her prickly legs off him. As he rounds the couch heading toward his office, he kisses the top of her head. "I love you, Woman."

Gretchen calls after her man, "If you loved me, Malcolm Price, you'd let me see Mama Girl's room."

"Tomorrow. Just give me one day."

Blue Marsh Lake

Layne Osterman has been lying low and licking wounds since her failed mission in Drexel Hill. No matter what Layne does, the first few lines of *I Feel Lucky* bang the fuck out of her head. When she's sleeping, when she's awake, even when she's at the firing range, the lyrics **bang** and **clang**. So far, the only reprieve from the noise is when she thinks deep about the time she spent in Alaska, and the time she spent beneath Eli when he came to inspect the readiness of the log cabin…

She stood just inside the tree line watching for signs of life in the log cabin. She knew someone was nearby, hadn't yet determined if the interloper were friend or foe. Movement passed the window from inside, "Looks like I've got company. Fucking should have taken my binoculars. Stupid mistake." She shifted her weight off her injured foot. "Goddamn puncture wound. Foot feels like it's on fire." She stepped behind a big-ass tree and removed her vest, turned it inside out to hide the neon bright orange. She parked her ass on a nearby rock and watched. Nearly an hour later he stepped outside. She pushed off the rock and began hobbling toward the cabin.

"It's about time, Layne," he met her halfway across an open field.

"Eli, give me a shoulder."

"What happened?"

"Stepped on a nail. I went to Urgent Care for a cleaning and a tetanus shot."

He pulled her into his arms, carried her inside, and set her on the couch. "Let me see."

"Medic Reynolds, it's way below your skill."

"Even so." He removed her boot, checked her foot, removed the rest of her clothes, and settled deep.

"What I wouldn't do to be in those woods, in that cabin, by the fire, or in the loft with him deep in me." After a minute of pining like some girly-girl she gets all up in her shit, "Fuck it all, Osterman, you're military, not some pussy sitting and waiting for a man to call. What you need is for your handler to call, granted they're the same man now, but forget he's the dick you want, and remember he's your boss."

Sarge joins her on her trek to the range, he reads her real quick, "You still stewing about the reporter besting you."

"Fuck you."

"Your handler would be fucking you with a bullet for failing your mission—course, he's fond of riding your pussy, Layne, so you've got that ace to play. Listen up. The truth is you didn't give enough mind to Staff Sergeant Meehan. She's Army like you. She used her training, found a fucking hole to hide in and stayed put. Can't kill something you can't scope, Osterman."

"I'll get the bitch one day, but that's not what's gotten me. I haven't heard from my handler. He knows I failed. Why hasn't he called?"

"He will. Right now, he wants you to squirm. It's his job to make sure you taste the bile of failure, that way you won't fail a second time. He's not done with you unless you fuck up again."

Layne stops moving and scowls at her host, "I will **never** fuck up again."

"Don't think you will."

Beaver Falls

Ten-year-old twins, Max and Josh Petty are where they're not supposed to be, deep in the woods surrounding their home in Beaver Falls, Pennsylvania. The boys had pushed their mother to her breaking point, so she sent them outdoors with a warning…

"Go find something to do outside, but stay close. Santa will know if you disobey and go deep into the woods. There'll be no presents under the tree tomorrow, but there'll be a tanning of your hides tonight if you venture too far."

The ten-year-old boys did what ten-year-old boys do—they trudged deep into the woods.

"We have to tell Mom and Dad."

"We won't sit for a week."

"Yeah, but there's bones in that burned car. We have to tell them."

"Wonder where they'll bury our bones when they kill us."

Alexandria

It's morning and Shelby **needs** coffee. The bugged briefcases are in the storage bin outside, so she does what she normally does when she first gets downstairs. She plugs in the coffee and she cranks Melissa Etheridge. She is belting, *I'm the Only One*, when John startles her from behind. He is exhausted and ornery, "Jack McGovern owes me big for keeping him from hearing you slaughter that perfect song."

"Insulting my singing is picking low hanging fruit, Director Maxwell. But then again, you've demonstrated your affection for trees with low hanging branches," she laughs.

"You're feisty this morning, Director Webber. Perhaps the clandestine moves of last night have invigorated you."

"Climbing trees, scaling walls, and dropping onto my property was fun, but we're in a mess of our own making. Let me recap for you. 1) We are supposedly in possession of a townhouse full of files and computers. 2) My second-in-command is a confirmed leader of a crime organization. 3) My home and office are bugged by listening devices. 4) I am bugged by a man who will not leave these premises."

John hops from the counter upon which he's been perched, "Are you finished?"

"For now."

"Good, because we have some pressing matters to discuss."

Shelby nods, "Proceed."

"1) We no longer need to drop a dime on Leavy's kidnapping. We can keep that information for another day. 2) We have Jack McGovern dead to rights as being part of The Realm. 3) The listening devices, the GPS trap, and the tails up my ass confirm that his role in The Realm is surveillance. 4) Someone in the organization torched the townhouses within 24-hours of our mentioning RFI's plan to go back in.

5) Mathis Reynolds is **not** going to be happy with Jack when he's told Stacy's stuff is supposedly in my possession."

"Director Maxwell, you already had a price on your head for your cyber defense skills, now The Realm thinks you're the only one who has access to Stacy's files and computers."

"Not the only one, ma'am. Jack knows I'm prohibited from making unilateral decisions in this matter. As far as he's concerned, I put the plan in motion, but you authorized the plan."

"Yes. You've upped the ante. The Realm will be gunning for both of us."

"I need a minute." He takes five. "We can't go to J. Edgar because our offices are bugged. We can't leave your briefcases outside for long periods of time, so that means we can't hang out here. We can't drive either of our GPS trapped vehicles. We have no reinforcements nearby. There's only one place where our safety is assured."

Shelby shakes her head, "I am not going to the Fiancetti Compound, John."

She is still shaking her head when they enter the forested fortress late Christmas Eve.

Christmas at The Compound.

John and Shelby trudge through beautiful snow-covered woods on their way to Christmas brunch at the Main Cottage. The guest cottage they've been assigned is on the outer perimeters, and the morning trek in frigid air has brought a beautiful rosy glow to Shelby's cheeks.

John takes a quick step in front of her, pulling her up short. He touches her cheek, waits to see if she moves away. When she does not, he takes her face in his hands, traces the contours of her cheekbones, along her chin, across her lips. "The dance between us has been fun, but we both know where this thing is headed. I want you, Shelby, and I'm quite sure you want me." He waits for her response. The wait is short.

"Yes, but—"

He leans in and kisses her before she finishes her sentence. The kiss is the kind that answers the heat of the moment—only to fan the flames of desire. He pulls her into his arms and wraps her there. "When we return to our cottage, you choose where you sleep."

The Main Cottage is filled to the rafters with RFI team members and their families. John is nearly tackled by his three daughters. After quick introductions to the younger two, Shelby spends some time with the Boy and Girl Genius. When Annie leaves, Shelby opines, "She'd be great at FICA."

"Why is that?"

"I can't get a read on her. I get smart, extraordinarily smart, but—"

John laughs, "Half the world thinks she's poodle-Annie, the other half thinks she's pit bull-Annie. I only see the pit bull."

Joy Fiancetti greets John with a laugh and a hug. "Pit-bull for sure. It's good to have you here. Relax a bit, then protect yourself when you return to DC."

John tilts his head in Shelby's direction, "You two must know one another?"

"We've met," they unison.

Joy repeats her sentiments, "I'm happy you made the trip, Director."

"Shelby."

"Ooo. Ooo. Gotta run." Joy moves away to scoop up a toddling boy who's making a run for the stairs leading to the loft, "Joseph, where do you think you're going?" She buzzes his neck. He giggles. She giggles.

"Joseph. He's the son of—"

The Toddling One's mother waves her hand, "Kitt Mahoney and Fred Serpico," the beautiful earth-momma answers as she makes her way into the arms of John Maxwell. "Christmas would not have been the same had you not come."

"Not much could keep me away, Kitt. Let me introduce you to Shelby."

Kitt smiles her million-watter, "You've chosen a wonderful place to spend Christmas. Is there anything I can get you two?"

John answers, "How about some of your Moscato for the wine connoisseur."

Kitt tosses another smile and calls back, "My Moscato is made for swigging, not for sipping, John."

Shelby laughs and offers to the retreating woman, "I think I'll need the swigging, Ms. Mahoney."

"Kitt," she calls over her shoulder.

"Good, Lord. That woman looks exactly like…"

"Evangeline Lilly," John and Fred unison.
Shelby laughs, "Yes."
"Except better," the men continue.
Shelby laughs heartier, "Yes."

Late afternoon ushers in gift-giving by the children. The gifts with any real significance are given out by Callie and Tess. They start with ones for their mothers. Callie hands a box and a card to Kitt and Tess hands the same to Joy. "Start with the boxes," they instruct.

"A UConn coffee mug?" Kitts chuckles.

"You told them UMass is the better school, right?" Joy asks as she holds her mug high.

"Open the cards and read them," they direct. The women read the front, **Christmas is full of wonder and of memories past ....** and then the inside, **And dreams of our future. Mom, we've been accepted at UConn and begin classes in January.**

Kitt whispers, "Accepted." Joy whispers, "Accepted." They both whisper, "Leaving?" Tears start flowing.

Callie and Tess go to their mother's rescue and address the group. "We finished our correspondence classes when we were in Laurel Falls with David Cluster and Jane Harper. We are high school graduates." A round of hoots and hollers fill the room. "Shhhhh, that's only part of it. We begin classes at UConn in January. The first semester will be online courses, but next fall we're gonna," the girls dribble imaginary basketballs across the floor as they unison, "bounce."

After the excitement dies down, Callie and Tess hand Fred and John long thin boxes similarly wrapped. "Dad, you first."

John opens the box, moves the tissue paper aside and cracks up laughing. He pulls his gift and announces, "A tuition and room and board bill for each of the girls." He reads the figure and roars in laughter. "Kitt and Joy, can I use your mugs? I need a stiff drink or two, and then I need to use them to bum for cash on the street corners."

Laughter abounds, and when it quiets again they encourage Fred, "It's your turn."

Fred opens the box, moves the tissue paper aside and cracks up laughing. He pulls an invoice from UConn that shows a zero balance on the girls' tuition and room and board bills. "Kitt and Joy, you get the mugs. John, you get the tuition bills. And I get to tell you that both girls received a full-ride basketball scholarship. Looks like you're off the hook, John."

This time, the room remains silent as the girls hold center court wrapped in their teary-eyed parents' arms.

There shouldn't be any gift-giving amongst the adults, but there is. Kitt Mahoney asks Joy Fiancetti and John Maxwell to join her at the

Christmas tree. She hands each a box, "Open them. It's my newest manuscript."

"*Netti Barn*."

Kitt moves close. "When I wrote *Bullet Bungalow*, I only told part of your story, John, and I wanted to pay respect to the other parts of your life—the important parts, the ones that define you. There was a great deal of anger when I first learned about your double life, but in writing *Netti Barn,* I ended at a place of understanding who we are, who we have always been—friends."

Kitt turns to Joy. "I couldn't tell John's story without telling yours. When you were reintroduced into my life it was not without pain and anger. But in many ways, I found it easier to make peace with you because you gave me the greatest gift—time with Tess. Joy I am profoundly humbled by your strength, inspired by your work, and grateful for your friendship. *Netti Barn* is as much your story as it is John's. I haven't sent this manuscript to my literary agent, and I will not publish it without your approval. Both Fred and Rocco have read excerpts and both agree that the choice is yours to make. No matter what you decide, this story is my gift to you, both."

John and Joy embrace Kitt and return to their seats speechless. The rest of the room remains in quiet reflection of a place called Netti.

Kitt and Fred take a sleeping Joseph and cooing Charlotte to their suite. Within minutes both babes are in their cribs dreaming of sweet nothings or dancing sugar plums.

Fred pulls his woman close, "I have something for you."

"I believe you already gave me something," Kitt nudges.

"And I will be giving that to you again in a few minutes. Until then why don't you open this, Kittridge?" Fred hands her a square black velvet box tied with a red satin bow.

She slides off the bow and opens the box. Set on red satin is a thin gold bangle. She takes it and slides her fingers across the smooth surface, stops when she finds the four channel set gemstones, one for each month of her children's births.

"Oh, Fred, it's beautiful. Truly, it's perfect." Kitt pulls it in for a closer inspection, "Oops, there's a problem with the gemstones."

"Don't even. I double and triple checked with Maura and she said—"

"They are the correct stones, Fred, there just aren't enough of them." Kitt remains silent while the detective figures out the mystery.

A Fred Serpico smile deep-dimples his face. He places his hand onto the beaming woman's belly, "Kittridge Mahoney, are you pregnant?"

"Merry Christmas, Fred Serpico."

Roman Emperor

Shelby is very quiet on the trek back to the cottage. The winter's cold and brilliant starry sky could be romantic, if one were aware of such things. The trekking woman concentrates on the trail and her need to make a decision. Does she join him in his bed, or…?

A cold blast of air follows them into a cold cottage. John heads to the fireplace to attend the dying embers. Shelby heads to her room.

"Seems you've made your choice, Shelby. I was hoping to move forward, but I'll wait," he whispers. As he passes Shelby's room he hears her shower running. He thinks about joining her, he doesn't.

Shelby shakes under the cold blast of water, "I cannot be in the same room with him, not if I'm to come to a clear-headed decision. And after tonight's merry-go-around of former lovers, now lovers, and new lovers, my head is spinning." She angrily pushes shampoo across her head, "It's like a damned cult," she mutters to herself. "Excuse me, but have we slept together? You look awfully familiar. Here read this book, it will help you remember if you've been in me." Shelby starts pulling threads. "John and Kitt. John and Joy. Fred and Kitt. Rocco and Joy. And don't get me started on the John-Leavy-Manuel saga. I think my head is going to explode."

She rinses and repeats into a full-blown lather. "It's a cult. Up in the middle of no-fucking-where, there's nothing but fucking." Shelby turns off the shower, wraps a towel around her body and another around her hair and storms to John's room.

He jumps at the intrusion.

"Exactly how many women have you bedded at this Compound of Caligula? No, don't answer that. Let me just tell you that there will **not** be another John Maxwell seduction at this den of iniquity. At least not one that includes me."

John moves toward Shelby.

"Don't take one more step John. I'm not done ranting, and while I do so, I want you over there."

He continues his advance, "Shelby."

"Don't say that!"

He stops a few feet from her. "The last steps are yours. Either enter my arms and my life, or leave."

Shelby enters his arms. "I'd better not end up as a chapter in a book that's given out next Christmas," she mutters before her lips are captured by his.

Christmas at 275.

Malcolm stations Randy and Peyton just beyond his bedroom suite, "Don't let Gretchen beyond this point. If she fights you, get Ted Brothers, he's armed."

Gretchen who is exiting the shower hears every word, "Run along, Mr. Mayor. There will be no need for gunplay in my home on Christmas morning." When she rounds the corner and takes a step toward Randy and Peyton, she is met with crossed arms and angry scowls. Gretchen is still muttering when she joins her guests in the living room. "Damned guards and armed men on Christmas morning. Merry fucking Christmas."

The clearing of her father's throat brings her back. "Sorry, Daddy. Fred must be somewhere near." She goes to her guests and pecks cheeks with cheery "Merry Christmas" greetings. The warm glow of tiny amber lights and the sparkle of ornaments beckon a lengthy stare at the lovely tree. Beneath the Blue Spruce are many more gifts than were there the day before. "What wonder, Santa came!" Gretchen gently rubs her baby ball, "Next year will be DelRae's first Christmas."

"She'll be moving all about by then, getting into everything—pine needles, tinsel, ornaments" Faye forewarns with a tone.

Gretchen's eyes widen, "Well, then, enjoy this tree because there will be no others. It's a damned deathtrap I tell you. It's a wonder any child can survive this holiday."

Malcolm and Mama Girl step off the elevator in time to hear the rant. "Who riled her?"

All hands point in Faye's direction.

"Would have liked to have seen that," he smiles wide at his decorating conspirator.

Gretchen squeals when she realizes Mama Girl has arrived, "Merry Christmas, Mama Girl! Now let's get you stripped of that outer gear. We have the most wonderful surprise for you. Well, Malcolm and Faye have a wonderful surprise for you because I've been banned from participation. So, you must settle quickly because I'm just about to burst." Gretchen motions everyone toward the hall. "Come, all of you. Now."

"Woman. You and Mama Girl sit on that couch and wait until you are called."

"Tyrant."

"Woman."

It's more than a few minutes before the two women hear the call from the most important man in each of their lives. They walk hand in hand to the doorway leading to the back half of the penthouse. Malcolm opens the door. "Gretchen, your surprise first." He leads her to DelRae's completely adorned nursery.

"Oh, Malcolm. The antique pink crib … the changing table and that rocker—they are simply beautiful. They are such a lovely contrast to the painted walls." She goes to the rocker and lifts a patchwork quilt. "I didn't choose this, but I most surely would have. It's gorgeous."

"I want you and DelRae *using* that. No saving it, you hear?"

"You made this, Mama Girl?"

"I did."

"It's…" The attention of the mother-to-be is pulled to a far wall. The words of A.A. Milne are calligraphed on the painted brick. Word for word, brick by brick. She steps near, "You are braver than you believe ~ stronger than you seem ~ smarter than you think ~ and loved more than you know. But the most important thing is, even if we're apart…I'll always be with you." Granger joins her and takes hold of her hand, "I learned those words by listening to your mother say them when she tucked you in at night. One day, you can tell DelRae how pleased her grandmother would be that they are in her room."

Gretchen's eyes sting with tears, "Daddy, you said those words to me on each of my birthdays ……. because my mother could not. I tell you, Granger Mitchell, you are a tender-hearted man, an imposter I should note. Not one living soul on this earth would have thought the man who wielded power and knowledge from behind a massive mahogany desk is nothing but a big, old, squishy…"

Granger wraps his arms around his daughter and takes a measure of pride and a moment of gratitude that a new chapter is being added to the Granger Mitchell and Delaney Rae Hamilton Mitchell story, the one he began so many years ago.

Complete silence takes hold of space and time in that nursery. It is many minutes before Gretchen finishes the tour. "I am overwhelmed. This is the most genuine moment of affection I have ever had and I will cherish this memory forever."

She moves to her husband, "Malcolm Price, I am the most blessed woman to be loved by you."

"There's more." Malcolm leads Gretchen and the merry band of elves to the finished playroom and points. "The baskets of stuffed animals, shelves of books, and building blocks, are from RFI, and in that corner…"

Gretchen walks toward a tiny desk with attached computer center upon which sits the world's smallest computer. Gretchen knows who the gift is from, but she reads the card, anyway. **To 78, From Uncle Randy and Auntie Peyton.** "I think I need to sit."

Malcolm sets his wife onto a rocker recliner then tends to the other woman in his life. He takes told of his mother's hand. "I hope you will make our home complete." He opens the door to the guest suite. Remembrance sweeps full as she recognizes the beautiful adornments of her room at Wyldwood Ranch. She is overcome with emotion.

"Mama Girl, the best gift Gretchen and I could ever give our little girl is you. We want you with us as we raise our baby. Please consent to joining us."

Malcolm's mother steps into the room. She moves slowly, running her hand across fluffy bed linens of yellow, pink, and green. She takes hold of one of the four posters on the queen-sized bed, then moves to the next. She picks up a tiny bud vase from an end table and smells the tiny bud that lives there. Next to a crystal footed potpourri bowl sits a familiar book. She smiles, "*Leaves of Grass* by Walt Whitman." She smiles as she opens it, the crack of the new spine pleases her. She reads the inscription on the inside cover,

Bertha, we hope your new home is filled with the love of family, the laughter of friends, and the time to enjoy poetry.
Fondly, Curtis and Madison.

Bertha moves to her son, "Bend down." She places a kiss upon his cheek, "This will be fine." With that, Mama Girl has a new home.

Randy and Peyton

The Kid and The Justice snuggle in front of the tree after all have retired for the evening. Randy talks softly against her hair, "Not feeling the Merry?"

The silence following Randy's question is broken by a long, deep pull of air and an exhaled, "I'm conflicted."

"About?"

"There are a million things I could do with my life. Right now, I am stuck between two options, playing it safe or…"

Randy interrupts her, "The opposite of playing it safe is not playing it safe, Peyton. Are you thinking about RFI?"

"Yes, but I'm thinking about us, too."

"Okay."

"Did you think about us before you made your decision to join RFI?"

Randy pushes up and spins Peyton toward him knowing this is the perfect time. "The Kid isn't ready for rings and things, Madam Justice, but I'm ready to make some commitments to you. That comment is mad ironic since ...." The Kid pulls a wedding ring from his pocket and hands it to Peyton.

She examines it, "This is a man's ring, a man's wedding ring."

"It's the ring I want you to give me when we do the whole matrimonial melding. Until then I want you to wear this." The hipster dude slips it onto the hipster chick's thumb. "Peyton Wells, would you be my non-fiancé?"

"Yes," the bow-lipped, square-faced, blue eyed Betty Boop beauty beams, "and I want to go on record saying that this is the coolest non-proposal proposal ever."

Penny and Ted

Penny slips into a funk when they get back to their apartment. The shit show life they've been sucked into robbed the couple of the joys of spending their first Christmas together. Ted picks up on her disappointment.

"Lucky. Hey, Lucky. You still with me? I know you're sitting next to me, but I think I lost you."

She sends him a smile that doesn't come anywhere near wrinkling the corners of her eyes.

Ted pulls her close. "I have, or had, something for you at the log cabin." Ted hoped his words would please her, but they have the opposite effect. "That gift was purchased before I realized how deep I am for you, Lucky. I see a life with you, and when I ask you to marry me, and I plan on doing just that, I want to do it up right. Since I can't do the whole marriage proposal right now, how about I ask you a different question?"

The smile on Penny's face crinkles all along her dark chocolatey eyes.

"That's my girl. So, the question is this: where will we honeymoon?" Ted kisses the top of Penny's head and whispers, "Marry Christmas."

Penny smacks him hard, "Tell me you did not just say **that**, Theodore Brothers."

"How about I tell you that I love you."

Christmas at Snowfall Prison.

Eli went heavy on Leavy's pills the night before, so it's late before she wakes, and when she does it is with a scream. He responds to her cry, finds her moving toward the edge of the bed, her back to the doorway.

"Are you—?"

"I'm fine. Are you cooking something?"

"Christmas dinner."

"It's Christmas." Leavy begins counting, trying to figure out how long she's been held captive.

Eli knows what she's doing. He answers her unasked question, "Sixteen days. We've been together sixteen days." He tosses the key onto the bed, "Unchain yourself and shower. Come back to the bedroom to get ready for the day. It is our first Christmas together."

Tears sting Leavy's eyes as she bends to put the key into the lock on her chains. When she returns to her bedroom she finds a red dress laid out on the bed. It is a sexy red dress. Her stomach churns as she pulls the sheath overhead and runs her hands down the silk. It looks better, sexier, than she imagined. She dies a little.

"You are stunning, Leavy."

She startles and turns to the doorway.

"Take your hair out of that bun."

She obeys. Her long mahogany hair falls in cascades down her back. A flash of Manuel holding a fistful as he entered her on their last time together cuts her deep.

"Dinner is almost ready and then I have a gift for you."

Leavy nods. "May I sit in the loft until dinner?"

"Of course." Eli steps back and lets her lead the way. When she is seated on her perch, he tosses her the key and she locks the chains. She leans against a windowsill, pulls her legs up onto the seat, and searches—for something, for anything, for a reason to survive.

After dinner Eli takes Leavy to the comfort room. "We are going to sit on the couch and talk. My gift to you is that I am not going to chain you. I slipped a mild relaxant into your dinner. It is strong enough to make it impossible for you to run, and it will help loosen you for things to come."

Her stomach churns. Her silent mantra begins. *An FBI agent does **whatever** it takes to survive.*

"We will be moving into our next phase, Leavy. I hope one day to have you as a partner, not a prisoner. This is our first step toward that." He takes her hand in his. "Tell me something about yourself. Anything you want to tell me. Keep in mind I know most everything there is to know, so don't lie to me."

Leavy sits for a moment. She's been suppressing her memories for weeks and finds it difficult connecting to her past. She rubs her hands along her bare arms. The movement unlocks something.

"I love to swim. My grandparents had a little red cabin on a lake. Crescent Lake. It's a beautiful pristine waterway that glistens in the day and gets lost into darkness at night. Their piece of land curved inward and made it so you believed the lake was all yours. It's very similar to the place in the movie, *On Golden Pond*. I loved the little red cabin at the lake. My grandparents let me name the camp when I was three."

Eli nods and smiles, "What did you name it?"

"Camp Winnie."

Eli pulls her onto his lap. Her tears begin. He touches her cheek and brushes away the tiny droplets. "You miss your grandparents."

"Yes." She hates herself for needing his comfort, tries to blame her weakness on the medication. She feels the hardness of his desire pulse beneath her. Fears that it is she who pulses with her desire. She tries to push away. Her mind is a mess, her body no longer her own. *Whatever it takes.* She might have said the words out loud. *No. Maybe.*

"Lift your dress and remove your panties," he directs. She is slow to move. "Leavy, don't ruin this evening," he warns. She moves off him and removes her panties. She lifts her dress up to her hips, he pulls it over her head. When she returns to his lap, he slides in. There is no resistance.

He fills her, feels her, releases her. She hates her body for betraying her, for betraying Manuel. *I don't want to survive.*

Christmas in Hell.

Felicity Ferraro has no desire to face the day. Her home has been desperately quiet since she sent her children away and she can't imagine what emotional horrors await her this Christmas morning. She begins the day the way she has for weeks: she mocks and berates herself. "You thought you were something. Thought you wielded power. Thought you had things under control. Thought you knew where your children were going. Well. You. Thought. Wrong. You have no power. You have lost all control. You have no idea where your children are. Worst of all, your husband, the father of your children is using them as weapons against you. And. You. Deserve. It."

The breaking woman tries to bury the thoughts of past Christmas mornings by burrowing beneath her bed pillow. "I wonder if anyone has committed suicide by suffocating themselves in bed." Hope abounds as she pulls the fluffy down pillow taut across her face. Anger pushes her from that endeavor and sends her to the en suite. She closes the bathroom door, though she need not, there is no one to see, or to knock, or to barge in. "I could spend the day here."

She heads to the shower, has a long cry that leaves her spent. "I was hoping for dead, but I'll accept exhaustion." On autopilot, she loofas, she shaves, she washes and conditions her long mahogany waves. She hums a Christmas tune until she realizes, then stops when she wonders if her little ones are singing the same song. "I wonder if anyone has ever committed suicide by drowning themselves in a shower." Hope abounds as she fills her mouth with water.

Still unmercifully alive, Felicity wraps her hair in a towel, throws on her terry robe and runs downstairs to fix a bite to eat. "Then it's back to bed to suffer through this wretched day." When she enters her kitchen she pulls up short.

"Felicity. It's about time you joined me."

"Mathis, I mean, Mr. Reynolds, what … how … what?"

The physically fit, impeccably dressed, handsome man of fifty walks to her, "You need better security. Make sure you get it. I want to be protected when I visit." He unwraps her hair and runs his fingers through the damp ends. He moves the terry cloth robe off one of her shoulders.

She blocks his hand, "I'm married."

"No, Felicity, you're widowed."

The End

More to come …

Please enjoy the teaser for my next book in the series,

Revenge…

REVENGE

THE ASSASSIN

--- PULLING THREADS ---

Book Fourteen

SHERYLL O'BRIEN

Christmas Wish List

Domination

Children

Freedom

REVENGE

ABOUT THE AUTHOR

She is not dead.

Sheryll O'Brien crafts characters without constraints. She tells them who they are, then let's them show her better versions of themselves. She gives them life and they live it beyond her wildest dreams.

Sheryll is a lifelong resident of Worcester, Massachusetts, where she is wife to the most supportive husband ever, and mother of two adult daughters, one who refuses to leave her home and the other who refuses to tell her where she lives. Of most significance, she is MammyGrams to the sweetest six-year-old, Hadley.

Sheryll worked several years in the fundraising community of Worcester County, writing grants for non-profit organizations. She began writing for her own pleasure after surviving brain surgery and breast cancer. Happily, for her fanbase of family and friends-—she is not dead.

If you have enjoyed reading my book, I would very much appreciate you taking a few minutes to write a review and post that review on amazon.com and goodreads.com.

The opinion of readers can help prospective readers make a purchasing decision.

To learn more, please visit my website, www.pullingthreadsnovella.com subscribe to my blog for updates on future projects.

I would absolutely love to hear from my readers, you can email me at,

pullingthreadsnovella@gmail.com

www.ingramcontent.com/pod-product-compliance
Lightning Source LLC
Chambersburg PA
CBHW070818180626
46818CB00001B/320